I HAVE DISCS, GET IN VAN!

Disc Golf Just Got Dangerous.

Written By Eric Mullaly

Staten House

EM&EM PUBLISHING

EST. 2024

Published by EM&EM Publishing
14 South 8th Street
Estherville, Iowa 51334

ISBN: 979-8-89496-395-2
Staten House
EM&EM Publishing

Library of Congress Control Number: 2025916376

Printed in the United States of America

First Edition: August 2025

Cover design by Emily Mullaly

Staten House

EM&EM PUBLISHING

Disclaimer: This is a work of fiction. Names, characters, places, and incidents either are products of the author's imagination or are used fictitiously. Any resemblance to actual events, locales, or persons, living or dead, is entirely coincidental.

Dedication

For my incredible family:

to my amazing wife and our wonderful kids,

thank you for your endless love, patience, and support.

You are my strength, my inspiration, and my reason for living.

This book would not exist without you.

— *Eric Mullaly*

WARNING: Urban Legend Alert

The tale you are about to read has been whispered about at disc golf courses across the country. Some say it started as a meme.

Others swear it's based on true events.

They say there's a white van that appears at random courses.

No license plate. No driver in sight.

Just a hand-scrawled sign that reads: *"I have discs."*

What happens when you step inside?

No one knows. Because those who do are never seen again.

This is the story of four friends. A bear. A neighborhood that was *too quiet*. Supernatural disc golf.

And something far darker than a water hazard.

You've been warned. Now flip the page... if you dare!

Table of Contents

Chapter 1: The Meme Made Real

Glenn is a tall, lanky young man, skinny yet muscular simultaneously, and very athletic, for he used to be a multi-sport star in high school. Upon arriving at the disc golf course, he notices a white van in the back of the parking lot, which appears to sell disc golf discs. The van has a spray-painted sign, "I have discs."

"Reminds me of the disc golf meme," he thinks as he looks for a parking spot. As Glenn pulls into the parking lot, a vague unease settles in his stomach. He recalls a story he'd once heard, an urban legend whispered among disc golfers about a white van that seemed to appear at random courses. The tale was simple: disc golfers would go to check it out, and they'd never be seen again. He'd always dismissed it as nonsense, but now, seeing the crude spray-painted sign that read 'I HAVE DISCS,' he couldn't shake the uneasy feeling.

A gust of wind blows some discarded flyers across the parking lot, one briefly pressing against his windshield before tumbling away. The paper was faded, the ink barely legible, but

Glenn swore he saw the word MISSING in bold letters before it disappeared. He shivers slightly but brushes it off as he parks his truck.

After parking, Glenn, dressed in his cargo shorts, disc golf shoes, disc golf shirt, and a hat, begins gathering all his disc golf gear as he gets ready to meet up with his friends Dina, Mateo, and Amy.

These aren't just any friends; they are his best friends, whom he's known for a long time now, and they do everything together. Dina is a ball-busting hard ass, yet a softy at the same time. She is taller than your average female, around 5'10", and athletic, for she used to wrestle in high school.

Amy is on the shorter side, only 5'2", but also athletic. Having been a jogger all her life and being a tremendous archer in high school, she has countless trophies for archery to show it. Mateo, on the other hand, was a baseball star in high school. Standing at 6', he is muscular and holds the all-time home run record for their former high school.

Having been those rare kings and queens of high school, all four of them also made everyone else feel like they were the kings and queens of high school. Never feeling like they were above anyone and always lifting those around them.

As Glenn steps out of his truck, he spots the others already gathering near the practice basket. "What's up, losers?" he calls out with a grin.

Dina rolls her eyes and says, "Big talk from the guy who hasn't beaten me in any round all year."

"Yeah, yeah," Glenn laughs, grabbing a putter and testing his grip. "Today's a new day."

Mateo winds up and flings a putt about 20 feet out, sinking it effortlessly. "Boom. That's what a champion looks like."

"Alright, showoff," Amy says, tossing a disc his way. "Let's see if you can back that up on the course."

The four continue warming up, tossing putters into the chains, and testing different angles and release points. Metal clanking fills the air as they compete to see who can make the most putts in a row.

"Alright, I'm calling it now. This is going to be my best round yet," Mateo says confidently.

Glenn smirks, shaking his head, "You say that every time."

The group lingers at the practice basket a little longer, warming up, stretching, and exchanging stories about their week. Glenn talks about a near miss he had on an ace last week, while Dina brags about finally getting her roller shot down. The conversation is easy, filled with laughter and teasing, as the four make their way toward the tee pad for hole one.

"Hey, look; someone is selling discs over there; want to check it out?" Amy asks the group as they all hang out on hole one.

"Maybe after the round," Mateo replies to Amy, with the others seeming to agree with his decision.

"Oh man, you guys hear about the dude who just won worlds, Kyle Rudd? Total unknown came out of nowhere and won it all with a close victory. It was crazy," Glenn asked everyone before they started their round.

"No, I haven't heard," Mateo responds. "I'll have to check that out tonight."

"Let's get our throw on!" With some enthusiasm, Glenn states he is excited to get a round-in with his buddies.

As they walk, Glenn's mind drifts back to the van. It still sits there, silent and still, but something about it just feels... off. He shakes his head, pushing the thought away. Today was about disc golf, friends, and good times. Nothing else.

Chapter 2: Tee Time Terror

The sun sits high in the sky, casting perfect conditions for a day on the course. A light breeze rustles the leaves overhead, and the faint hum of cicadas fills the air. Other disc golfers chat in the distance, their voices blending with the occasional clang of chains being hit. It's the perfect day to play. The group approaches tee one, each selecting their first disc.

"Alright, who's feeling confident?" Glenn asks, lining up his shot.

"Not you," Dina quips, smirking. "But let's see if you can at least keep it on the fairway."

"Damn, already with the trash talk," Glenn laughs as he lets his disc rip. It glides smoothly down the fairway before settling just shy of the basket. "That's how it's done."

Mateo whistles. "Not bad, not bad. But let me show you how a real athlete does it.

He steps up, takes a deep breath, and launches his drive. The disc sails beautifully, skipping off the ground and stopping mere feet from Glenn's. "And that's why I'm the king."

Amy gives a slow clap. "Alright, boys, nice throws. But don't let it get to your heads."

The group continues playing, enjoying their casual competition, laughing and teasing each other throughout the round. Glenn gets an easy birdie on hole two, while Dina smirks as she manages an even longer putt to match him. Mateo groans after his approach shot catches the edge of a tree, leaving him with a tough par save.

"That tree was totally in my way," Mateo grumbles, shaking his head.

"It's always the tree's fault," Amy teases as she lines up her throw. "Let's see if I can do any better."

Amy flicks a smooth forehand shot and watches the disc curve perfectly around the trees, landing within ten feet of the basket. She gives the boys a victorious grin. "You guys are really making this too easy for me."

"Alright, alright, we get it," Glenn chuckles. "Next hole, we're stepping it up."

On hole four, Glenn attempts an ambitious roller shot, but it catches an unexpected slope and veers wildly off course. Dina and Mateo burst out laughing as he throws up his hands in frustration.

"Okay, note to self," Glenn mutters, retrieving his disc. "Stick to the air shots."

As they make their way toward hole five, Glenn catches Amy glancing toward the van again. This time, she seems more focused, as if trying to make out movement from the corner of her eye. He considers asking about it but decides against it, chalking it up to her curiosity.

"Alright, hole five," Mateo announces, stretching. "Let's see who's got the arm for this one."

The group moves along, enjoying the rhythm of the game. Each hole brings a new challenge, some tight wooded fairways that demand precision, others wide open where power throws are center stage. On one particularly tricky hole, Glenn threads a perfect shot through a narrow gap in the trees.

Smash! As the disc hits the chains and falls into the basket. Being less than halfway into their round, having a good shot already felt great for Glenn.

"I can't believe that made it through," Glenn says, shaking his head. "It's almost like I meant to do that."

"Great shot," you can hear a player call out from a distance.

"Did you just make that?" You can hear another player asking from another hole, not even a part of the group.

"Yeah, I can't believe it went in," Glenn replies, walking up to clear his disc from the basket.

"That was an amazing shot, dude. How far out were you?" The player from another hole asked Glenn.

"I'd guess around 130 feet; I had to weave it through the trees, too. It's why I can't believe I drained it; it was a blind shot."

"Great one, man. Well, have a great rest of your round. My name is Jonah, and I'm a local here; if you ever want to throw a round, I'm usually out here most days around this time. Again, great shot. I'm glad I got to witness it," Jonah says as he readies to head back to join his group.

"My name is Glenn; I'm new to this course, so I'll have to hit you up on that offer sometime. You have a good round yourself. Take it easy!" Glenn replies as he, too, readies to head back to join his group.

The group continues playing, enjoying their casual competition, laughing and teasing each other throughout the round, but Glenn can't quite shake the feeling that something, or someone, is watching them.

Chapter 3: The Van Revisited

The sun dips lower as they finish their round, stretching long shadows across the course. Glenn stretches his arms, feeling the wear of the game settling into his muscles.

"Well, that was a solid round," Mateo says, slinging his bag over his shoulder. "I could use a drink. Anyone up for a stop at The Rusty Putter?"

Dina nods. "I could go for a beer."

"I think I'm going to check out those discs before heading out," Amy announces, eyeing the van.

Glenn follows her gaze. The white van sits motionless in the parking lot, the same as before, yet something about it feels... different.

"You sure?" Glenn asks. "That thing gives me bad vibes."

Amy rolls her eyes. "Oh, please. It's just some guy selling discs. You all go have fun. I'll catch up."

Mateo drives away, he honks his car horn and hollers, "You good, Amy?"

Amy waves him off. "Yeah, just checking some discs out real quick."

As Glenn loads his truck, he keeps an eye on her as she approaches the van. The slightly ajar door creaks open just a bit more as she nears. A faint rustling sound carries through the evening air. Was it the wind? Or something else?

She gives them a wave before approaching the van, her pace slowing slightly as she nears. Glenn watches as she hesitates at the threshold, peering inside. The van looks almost too dark inside, almost as if the shadows swallowed the light. Something about the scene makes the hairs on his neck stand up.

Amy hesitates at the threshold. "Hello?" she calls out.

Silence. She glances over her shoulder at Glenn, offering a casual shrug before stepping forward.

Glenn frowns. Something about it still feels off to him. The shadows around the van seem darker than before, stretching unnaturally. His gut tells him to call Amy back, but she's already stepping up to the van, peering inside.

She glances over her shoulder at Glenn, offering a casual shrug before stepping forward. Then, the door swings open just a little wider, and Amy disappears and screams. Glenn jumps and starts running for the van before Amy pops back out, laughing and waving at Glenn. "Got you!"

"Ha. Ha. Very funny, Amy!" shaking his head, Glenn turns around and drives off in his truck.

Chapter 4: Captured by Chains

As Amy watches her other two friends leave, waving goodbye, she heads to the white van. Upon getting close to the truck, she doesn't see anyone around.

"Hello, anyone there?" Amy says, with some volume in her voice, as she's totally confused as to why no one is here. She starts walking even slower up to the van, looking around everywhere to see if she sees anyone associated with the vehicle.

"Feel free to check out discs. I'll be back shortly."

Amy notices the handwritten sign, appearing to have been written in a strange substance on an old piece of raggedy cardboard.

"I guess I'll start looking until the owner arrives," Amy thinks to herself as she looks inside the van. The discs are all up on custom-built shelves inside the van, leaving no choice but to step in to be able to check them out thoroughly.

She hesitantly and slowly climbs into the van, allowing her love for disc golf, checking out discs, and trusting fellow disc golfers to drop her guard completely. As soon as she climbs all the way in the van to check out the discs, the doors close abruptly, trapping her inside. A weird powder-looking substance starts being pumped into the van. Instantly holding her breath, Amy begins to look for a way out right away, banging on the doors she just stepped through.

With a custom-built wall blocking her from getting into the driver's seat and another custom-built wall blocking the back doors, she finds herself completely trapped inside, with all the walls covered in disc golf discs. The only way out is the way she came in the door is solidly secure with no handles or buttons to open the door back up.

Trapped in the van with no way out, a mysterious powder fills the back of the van. Unable to hold her breath for any longer, Amy is forced to inhale the strange powder, immediately passing out.

"What the hell?" Amy asks as she starts to come too. "What the hell is going on?" She begins to look around as starts to come to and her blurry vision begins to focus.

Bang.

Bang.

Bang.

Amy pounds on the walls in a panic trying to get someone to help her. "Is anyone there?" She yells out. "Please help me!"

"Shh, they'll hear you," a strange voice calls back out to her.

"Who will hear me? Where are we? What's going on?"

"Please be quiet, or they'll hurt you," the strange voice says back.

As Amy tries not to panic fully, she realizes she still has a lighter on her. Her kidnappers appeared to have taken everything out of her pockets, but they missed a little pocket on the inside of Amy's zip-up hoodie that she was wearing. Trying to find something to light on fire so she can try and see where the strange voice is coming from, Amy sets her sights on the mattress she woke up on that was lying on the floor.

She rips a clump of cloth from the mattress and balls it up the best she can to help it stay lit longer. As soon as Amy gets it in a ball, she begins to try and light it on fire in hopes of tossing it out the door to the room since it has an opening protected with bars, hopefully being able to get her arm through the bars.

Amy can't tell exactly how far away the voice is, but she hopes to get a lucky toss and light up enough of the area to see. She lights up the cloth ball and throws it, watching as the hallway lights up with the flames allowing her to see that it's a longer hallway with only a few rooms. They all appear to have the same type of door as hers. The flames light up even more of the hallway, and that's when she sees the source of the strange voice coming from another jail cell.

"Hello," the man says as he steps into the light. The man appears to be very large and extremely filthy, as if he has been in here for a long time, in what seems to be an actual dungeon of some sort.

"Oh my, are you okay?" Amy asks the man.

"Yes, they feed us plenty," he replies.

"How long have you been down here?" Amy asks as her curiosity begins to take over.

"I don't know exactly, maybe a few weeks. We can't tell when it's day or night, and they took everything from us upon arrival. All we get is all the food we want. They feed us massive meals once a day that lasts all day," the man answers. "Are you a disc golfer too?"

"Yeah?" Amy responds, thinking to herself, "What the hell is going on here?"

Suddenly, they hear a sizeable creaky door opening with a loud squeal worse than nails on a chalkboard.

"Shhh, don't make them mad," the man tells Amy as he slips into the back of his cell.

The lights then go on, and everyone in the dungeon can hear the sound of multiple people walking down the stairs, reaching the bottom, slowly getting closer to Amy's cell, one sinister sounding foot step at a time.

When they stop in front of her cell, Amy finally gets a good look at the kidnappers and gasps, "What the hell are you?"

Chapter 5: The Van Returns

Beep. Beep. Beep.

Glenn's alarm goes off, waking him up and forcing him to turn it off. Instead, though, Glenn decides to hit his snooze button to get a little more sleep.

Beep, beep, beep.

There it goes again Glenn groans as he reaches over and hits the snooze button.

Beep, beep, beep.

This time, groaning but finally moving, Glenn knows he can't lay in bed any longer, it is time to get up and start his day. He sits up in bed, groggy, and drinks the water he sleeps with beside his bed on the nightstand. After a couple of gulps, Glenn picks up his phone to see what he missed during the night. To his surprise, there are several missed texts and calls.

From Dina, "Have you heard from Amy? She never came home last night."

From Mateo, "Dude, this is weird. Any word from Amy? This isn't like her."

The texts continue, and both Dina and Mateo express their concern for their friend, Amy. Glenn begins to send a group text to both at the same time.

"Is it possible she went to the bar last night and hooked up with somebody?"

While waiting for a response, Glenn puts his phone down and begins to get ready, for he and his friends have plans to hit up a different disc golf course on the day.

The phone begins to vibrate.

It's another text from Dina, "That is a possibility; it doesn't happen much, but it does happen sometimes."

Glenn begins to text back, "Well, let's get out and throw, and maybe she'll still meet us out there."

As he's putting his shoes on and gathering up his disc golf bag, his phone vibrates again with a response from Dina, just giving Glenn a thumbs-up emoji. Glenn then puts his phone away and finishes getting ready to head out to disc golf with his friends.

While grabbing his bag, he begins looking through all his discs to ensure they are all there and contemplating swapping any out. Glenn's bag consists of various brands, including Prodigy, Latitude 64, Discmania, Discraft, and Innova.

Upon arriving at the disc golf course, Glenn immediately notices the white van in the back of the parking lot, the same white van from yesterday for Glenn recognizes the spray-painted sign "I have discs."

Once again, Glenn can't help but think about the famous disc golf meme, "What's the number one way to kidnap a disc golfer?" And on the picture shows a white van with a sign stating, "I have discs."

Dina and Mateo soon show up, and they all get on with their round. Today, they're playing another course they've never played before, and this course is extra woodsy.

"You guys know what, this course sort of reminds me of the course where we had to fight that bear," Dina started reminiscing about the crazy time and memory they all shared.

"Oh yeah, you're totally right!" People still don't believe that ever happened or think I embellished the story's facts," Mateo responds.

"I'm not surprised. I barely believe it happened, and I was there," Glenn says jokingly.

"Craziest day of my life, by far," Dina states, with Mateo and Glenn nodding in agreement.

Sometimes the truth is stranger than fiction!" exclaims Mateo.

All of them pause for a moment as they gaze into the distance collectively remembering that crazy day.

Chapter 6: Bear on the Fairway

It was a perfect Saturday morning, and the sun peeked through the tall pines lining the edges of Pine Hill Disc Golf Course.

Glenn, Amy, Dina, and Mateo were out for their weekly disc golf game. The air was crisp, the sky was clear, and the course was virtually empty, just how they liked it.

Glenn stepped up to the tee pad on hole 7, a challenging par 4 with a narrow fairway cutting through the dense woods. He lined up his shot, took a deep breath, and launched his favorite driver, the disc slicing through the air with a satisfying whoosh.

"Nice throw!" Dina exclaimed as they watched the disc soar.

As they walked down the fairway, enjoying the tranquility of nature and discussing their latest disc purchases, a sudden rustling in the bushes ahead caught their attention. Out of the thick underbrush emerged a massive grizzly bear, its eyes locked onto them with an unsettling intensity.

"Whoa! Bear!" Amy shouted, her voice a mix of surprise and fear.

The friends froze, heartbeats quickening as the bear took a menacing step forward, growling low and deep. They had read about bear encounters before, but experiencing one firsthand was a different story. The bear's fur was bristled, and its ears were pinned back, signs of aggression they had learned about. They knew they had to act fast.

"Okay, no sudden moves," Glenn said quietly, trying to recall the advice he'd read online about bear safety. But as the bear reared up on its hind legs, it became clear that this bear wasn't interested in backing down.

Without warning, the bear charged. Mateo, thinking quickly, took the disc he was holding and flung it at the bear, hitting it square on the nose. The bear roared in anger but hesitated for a moment.

Glenn saw his opportunity. "We've got to confuse it and make it retreat," he shouted. He grabbed his disc and hurled it at the bear's head. The bear growled and swiped at the disc, its attention divided.

Inspired by the quick thinking, Amy and Dina joined in. Amy spun around, using a powerful disc throw to hit the bear's flank, while Dina reached for a different approach. She yelled, "Wrestling moves, remember your wrestling moves from when we used to watch WWF and WCW!"

Mateo, who used to love watching wrestling on TV, nodded. As the bear stepped forward, he darted to the side and delivered a well-timed double leg kick to its hind leg. The bear stumbled but quickly regained its footing. Glenn followed up with a running shoulder tackle, aiming for the bear's side, his body slamming into it with all his might. The two ladies quickly followed up with a double clothesline maneuver.

Glenn and Mateo then climbed onto branches on both sides of the bear and delivered elbow drops, with Amy and Dina delivering body splashes next.

The coordinated attack bewildered the bear. Armed with her favorite mid-range disc, Dina aimed for the bear's eyes, throwing the disc with precision. It skimmed past, just close enough to cause the bear to blink and shake its head in confusion.

Not one to be left out, Amy recalled a move she'd seen in a wrestling match. She ran up and leaped onto the bear's back, wrapping her arms around its neck in a chokehold. The bear roared and shook, trying to throw her off. Glenn and Mateo quickly joined in, grabbing at the bear's legs and using all their strength to bring it down.

With a final, mighty roar, the bear shook free and retreated into the woods, defeated and bewildered by the unexpected assault. Peaking back with a sort of confused look in its eyes as if the bear couldn't believe what had just happened.

The friends, their hearts still pounding and adrenaline surging through their veins, exchanged bewildered looks before a wave of relief washed over them. It was a moment that would forever remain etched in their memories, a testament to the extraordinary courage and unity they showed in the face of imminent danger. The friends stood there, panting and wide-eyed, adrenaline coursing through their veins. They stared at each other in disbelief before bursting into laughter. It was a moment they would never forget and no one would ever believe.

"Did that just happen?" Amy asked, still catching her breath.

"It sure did," Glenn replied, picking up his scattered discs. "And we just took down a bear with pro wrestling moves and disc golf discs. I think that deserves some kind of award."

"Well, there's still a round to finish," Mateo said, grinning. "We can't let a little bear attack ruin our game."

They gathered their discs, dusted themselves off, and continued down the fairway, resuming their game as if nothing had happened. They played the rest of their round with a renewed sense of camaraderie and an unforgettable story.

Chapter 7: Into the Dungeon

As the round continues, the group of friends can't help but bring up their friend Amy, wondering where she could be and what she could be doing. It's not like her to miss a round of disc golf with her buddies like this. Things just weren't sitting right with the group. They start discussing a plan to locate her, but they can only think of going around to all the bars with a picture.

However, being in a big city, there are just too many bars to make that possible. The group then decides to at least check the two bars they tend to go to as a group and ask around. They finish their round, head to their cars, load up their gear, and proceed to try to locate their friend.

"I'll go check out the bar on Main Street," Glenn tells the group as he packs up his disc golf gear.

"I'll go check out the one on 5th Street," Dina replies while packing her disc golf gear into her van.

"Alright, that sounds great. Please hit me up after you check out both bars, so I know what's going on. Even if you don't find anything out, let me know anyway," Mateo says to everyone as he thinks about going and checking out the van selling discs. "Since you two seem to have this, I'm going to check out the van while I'm here and see if they got any sweet discs I'd like."

"If you see a sweet Prodigy 500 F3, let me know. I'm always on the lookout," Glenn lets Mateo know as he starts up his vehicle, getting ready to head out to the bar.

"Will do!"

Mateo waves Glenn off and then proceeds to head over to the van. As Mateo walks closer to the van, he can see all the discs on display, but no one is around. The same sign his friend Amy saw the day before is again on display.

"Feel free to check out discs. I'll be back shortly."

He then proceeds to step up to the van to check out the discs. With them inside, he steps into the van to take a closer look at them. The van doors immediately close and lock him in;

the van then begins to shake as if Mateo is trying to escape, then suddenly stops moving.

Sometime later, Mateo wakes up, "Whoa, what the hell happened?" he quietly says aloud as he slowly starts coming too. "Where am I?" he says while looking around, panicking at the sight of the strange and dark surroundings.

"Hello!" Mateo begins to yell out, "Is anyone there?"

Suddenly, a familiar female voice calls back to him, "Mateo, is that you?"

Mateo, feeling a slight bit of relief, calls back out, "Hey, I know that voice. Amy, that's you, isn't it?"

"Holy crap, yeah, it's me. How did you end up here?" Amy calls back out.

"We met up today to go throw as planned at the new course, and the same white van from the course yesterday was there, so I went to go check out discs. I stepped into the van to look at the discs, and the next thing I knew, I was waking up in this cell. How did you end up here and where is here?

"After we played yesterday, I, too, went to check out the van, and the doors closed on me, and a weird powder-like substance filled up the van, knocked me out, and I woke up here. I don't know where we are, but they are feeding us tons of food here. Good, too, like exceptionally good, the best food I've ever had in my life. They haven't hurt me or anyone that I've seen yet. There appear to be several people locked up in cells up and down a hallway we are a part of.

All the people are quite large and are gaining weight quickly and none of them were large when they originally arrived, they explained to me. It's bizarre and very frightening. Oh, and get this, they are all disc golfers too. I've been trying to figure a way out, but no luck so far," Amy starts explaining to Mateo about everything she's experienced over the past nearly 24 hours.

"Wait, what? They are feeding everyone tons of good food. That's the weirdest thing I've ever heard. Is everyone trapped here disc golfers? Who are these people who kidnapped us? Why are they doing this?" Mateo asks back.

"I don't know, but they don't look normal," Amy responds.

"What do you mean?"

"They look like…"

Just then, the lights came on, and footsteps walking down the stairs echoed.

Amy then whispers to Mateo, "Shhh, just be quiet and try to see for yourself."

Chapter 8: Flashback by the Lake

"Can we get two beers, please?" Glenn lets the waitress know what they would like.

"So, have you heard from Amy yet? And now Mateo is late meeting us here, too. What the hell is going on?" Dina, starting to grow weary, asks Glenn.

"I haven't heard from either; it's starting to freak me out," Glenn responds back. "Should we be going to the police?"

"What would the police do? I don't think they've been missing long enough; we aren't family, and they'll probably just tell us they'll turn up when they want. We may need to figure this out ourselves," Dina states, not putting much faith in the police.

As the two friends sit there, they start trying to figure things out. First, they try to figure out if the two did anything that may have been in common with the other. That's when it dawns on Dina.

"The white van!" Dina randomly says. "They both wanted to go check out discs at the weird white van at the courses we were at. Do you think that van could have anything to do with them missing?"

"Only one way to find out!" Glenn exclaims, entirely in agreement with Dina.

Right away, they plan to meet up in the morning to go out looking for the white van. Seeing how it was at two different courses, two days in a row, it doesn't help them much to know where to start checking due to how many disc golf courses there are in the area. Since the two courses they were on are both on the west side of town and slightly outside of town, they decide to check the other courses in that area first, hoping to have some luck locating the van.

Dumbfounded at the possible kidnapping of their best friends, they part ways from the bar before finishing their drinks ready to go out and look for them. Glenn heads straight to his vehicle, climbs in, and begins to break down a little bit, for all this has started to bring back some dark memories.

Several years back, when he was a teenager, he was at a local lake beach with his little brother when his little brother went missing. Since his little brother was last seen out in the water, officials determined that he drowned, even though a body was never found.

According to the search and rescue teams, many bodies aren't found in this lake due to all the crevices and large rocks at the bottom of the lake. Glenn always suspected that his brother did not drown but was kidnapped somehow by someone who took him out of the water and off that beach.

After sitting there for a while, thinking of that nightmarish day, Glenn finally drives off and heads home. That night, he tosses and turns, rolling in the bed, unable to fall asleep. Unable to sleep after hours of trying, he remembers that horrible day...

"Hey Garrett, ready to head to the lake?" Glenn yells across the house, seeing if his little brother is ready to go.

With Glenn being 19 when it happened and his little brother Garrett being only 11, there was quite an age difference between the two, but that didn't stop either of them from being best friends with each other.

Being the kids of a single dad, since their mom died when Garrett was little, Glenn has not only been a big brother but almost another parent to his little brother.

Their dad works a lot to pay the bills, and on top of that, he has to commute for more than hour to reach work, taking even MORE time out of his day away from his kids. So, to help his dad out, Glenn is the main one who cooks, cleans, and helps with Garrett around the house while their dad supports them. All three of them have been working as a team since the passing of their mom.

"Yeah, I'm ready. I'm just grabbing my inner tube and a few discs," Garrett responds to his older brother.

Floating on their tubes at the lake is one of their favorite things to do during the warm months, along with disc golf, both activities the brothers frequently do together.

After grabbing his tube, Garrett heads to the car, where his brother awaits him. They then head straight to the beach.

Upon pulling up to the beach, they can see it is extra crowded on the day. So, they pull into the parking lot, attempting to find a parking space, but fail to do so, making them park up the road. Unfortunately, the road is even filled with cars, all up and down, forcing the brothers to park very far away.

After searching and finally finding a spot, then parking, they get out of the vehicle and begin to gather their stuff. Much to Garrett's surprise, Amy comes up and greets the two brothers.

"What's up, you two?" Amy surprises them both with her question.

"Heyyyy, Amy!" Garrett says excitedly, running up to Amy and giving her a big hug. "Are you hanging with us today?"

"Why, yes I am, big guy," Amy responds back.

After having to park so far away, the three gather up all the stuff they pulled out from Glenn's car and start the trek to the beach. When they finally arrive at the beach, they have the next task of finding a spot to lay down their towels and stuff they brought with them.

Weaving their way through the crowd of sun-soaking beachgoers for what seems like an eternity, the three finally locate a spot to lay out. After laying all their stuff down and setting up their spot, Garrett is ready to head to the water.

"Come on, come on, let's go get in the water," Garrett pleads to his brother, not wanting to wait any longer to swim and float on his tube.

"Go ahead and head down to the water, and we will be there shortly," Glenn responds to his little brother as he finishes blowing up his and Amy's innertubes. "Just be careful out there!"

Garrett then runs off to the water with his tube around his arm.

"I can't believe how strong your little brother is," Amy starts talking to Glenn. "He's handled your mom's death like a champ!"

"He sure has; it also really helps how much you've been there for us, Amy. I'm not sure we could be doing this well without you. You truly are a remarkable friend." Glenn explains to Amy.

"It's my pleasure; you two are like family to me, and your parents are the parents I never had," Amy replies.

Amy never knew her parents, for she was put into foster care from a very young age and bounced around homes all her life until she settled in the city, which they all currently live in.

Glenn finishes blowing up their innertubes. Then, the two proceed to head down to the water to meet up with Garrett. After what feels like trying to weave through lasers to break into a bank vault, the two finally make it through the throngs of people down to the water, where they immediately locate Garrett's inner tube out in the water, but no Garrett is in sight. Glenn starts to get a little brush of panic throughout his body.

"Garrett!" Glenn yells out.

"GARRETT!" He calls out even louder.

He quickly starts to panic even more and starts looking off frantically in all directions, inspecting every group out on the water in hopes of seeing his little brother. Just then, Garrett comes jumping out of the water from the center of his innertube. Glenn and Amy immediately rush over to him.

"You scared the crap out of us, Garrett," Glenn says to his brother.

"Sorry, I was just swimming underwater for a little bit," Garrett explains where he was.

"You had us a little scared there for a second; with how many people are here today, anything can happen," Amy chimes in. Well now that is over, let's have a fun day on the lake!"

The three of them then proceed to have an incredible day on the lake together. Swimming, floating, building sandcastles, the perfect day in all of their eyes. Amy even brought a picnic for all of them to enjoy, even making Garrett his favorite peanut butter and banana sandwiches.

Then, the time came to head out after spending hours upon hours out on the water. Since it was towards the end of the day for them, Glenn and Amy were lying down on the floating dock while Garrett floated on his tube around them chattering away, talking their ears off.

Then, after a little bit of silence from his little brother, Glenn, lying down, begins to sit up and call out to his little brother, "Alright, Garrett, time to head out, buddy." He looks around for his little brother and immediately notices his innertube, but no Garrett. Assuming it was like before, Glenn sat there and waited for Garrett to surface. Only this time, Garrett doesn't surface.

"Wait, what the hell, GARRETT?" he yells, "GARRETT, ANSWER ME!"

No response. Both he and Amy begin to panic and shout out at everyone if they've seen Garrett, but no luck. They start to search everywhere, including diving underwater and searching there, but they still cannot locate Garrett. They call the police and continue looking everywhere while they show up.

Police show up almost immediately, for they must have been in the area, and begin combing the entire area, including calling in divers to search the lake. After hours of answering questions and looking, the police send Glenn and Amy home.

In the end, the lake has all sorts of large rocks and crevices at the bottom, and the police believe the boy sank to the bottom and got stuck under one of them, declaring his brother an accidental drowning. However, that never sat well with Glenn, for he always felt that foul play was at hand and that his brother was taken by someone, somehow. For he could feel he was alive, at least for a while after the disappearance.

After a long night of not sleeping well, tossing and turning, dreaming about the last day he spent with his brother, Glenn wakes up to the sound of his alarm.

Beep, beep, beep!

As the alarm clock beeps for Glenn's 7 am alarm. He doesn't hesitate to get up this morning, for he and Dina need to go out searching for the white van with the spray-painted sign "I have discs" on it. After quickly getting ready and grabbing a quick breakfast and a cup of coffee, Glenn texts Dina to let her know he is ready.

"Hey, Dina, I'm ready to head out. Are you coming to pick me up?"

It doesn't take long for Glenn to get a response from Dina, letting him know she will be there in 10 minutes. While waiting, Glenn runs across one of the pictures on his wall, which is of himself, Amy, and Garrett, at the beach one day. It was not the same day his brother disappeared, but another day like it, one with much happier memories. After staring at the picture for a bit, he begins to break down a little while reminiscing about all the wonderful times he had with his little brother while he was still around.

"How is this happening again?" He says out loud to himself. Remembering how he never once believed that his little brother drowned.

After he loses track of time, thinking of all the good memories of him and his brother, he hears Dina honking her horn to get his attention. Glenn heads out the door and hops in the car with Dina. The two start making their plan to locate the white van.

Chapter 9: Hunt for the White Van

"Alright, we need to find that van, so where do we start?" Dina asks Glenn once he gets settled in her vehicle.

"Let's start with where it was yesterday and go from there. If it's not there, we can go check the course the first time we saw it," Glenn answers back.

They two set out for the course they went to the previous day. Pulling into the parking lot, they do not see the white van. After they sit for a bit, waiting, but with no luck, they proceed to the other course, where they saw the van once before. It takes them about 10 minutes, but they arrive at the course, and once again, with no luck, there is no van.

"Alright, we need to figure out all the courses in the area and start checking them out," Glenn says in disappointment, hoping the van would've been at one of the two courses they checked out and where it was previously spotted.

The two begin plotting out the best route to start checking out all the disc golf courses in the area. One by one, they check each course, and one by one, they have no luck locating the white van. Several hours pass while searching, and by now, the two of them are starting to get frustrated at their lack of luck.

"Alright, for giggles, let's go back and check out the first two courses again, just in case," Dina suggests after they just checked out their final course on the day.

"Yep, I'm down," Glenn replies. "Couldn't hurt at this point since we've had no luck so far."

So, the two of them head on over to the course from yesterday, and yet again, no luck.

"Damn it," Glenn says as they pull into the parking lot, once again having no luck finding the van. "Alright, let's check out the other course again, and if there's no luck, we'll just have to try again tomorrow, I guess."

They make their way to the other disc golf course, and along the way, they start talking about all the good times they spent with the four of them. Once again, bringing up their infamous bear story. All the good times they've had hanging out, playing video games, disc golfing, having drinks, watching movies, and just talking with each other. After all, they were all best friends, like family to one another. After some time, they made their way back to the first course. They pull into the parking lot, and to their surprise, the van is there!

"Hell yeah, we found it!" Dina says excitedly.

After pulling into the parking lot, they look for a spot and find one, keeping a distance from the van to keep an eye on it. By this time, it was around 5 pm in the evening, but disc golfers were still out in abundance. One by one, they watch disc golfers go up to the van and purchase discs from what appears to be just a normal-looking person with no bad vibes whatsoever.

"What the hell is going on? This doesn't look shady at all," Glenn, puzzled, says to Dina.

"Yeah, I agree," Dina replies. "I guess let's just keep watching and see if anything changes. I mean, it couldn't hurt. We have no other leads. I am starting to doubt if this is how they disappeared, though, not gonna lie."

The two continue to sit there, watching the van, with still no shady-looking behavior at all. It appears that people are even buying discs and walking away with new plastic. Hell, they are even selling buzzsaw Buzzz by the looks of things, as they see an excited patron walking away with a purchased one.

After a few hours of watching, the sun starts to go down, leaving only a few disc golfers out on the course, judging by how many vehicles are left in the parking lot. However, the pair remain there, sitting, waiting, and watching for anything to happen. After a little bit more time passes the pair can see the person with the creepy van begin to pack up.

They continue to watch the driver just in case, but still nothing seems off. The van then starts to drive directly in front of them, both Dina and Glenn looking right at the driver as he goes by; the driver then turns and looks at them with the most sinister-looking grin on his face. The grin was so evil, as if in no way it could've been the person they'd seen driving, almost as if another person was inside the person. Sending chills down both their spines, Dina immediately turns on her vehicle and follows the white van.

Left turn, right turn, the van seems to be driving with no set direction in mind. Just then, they realize that they've circled back and are heading back in the same direction as the course they just left. However, instead of turning into the park where the course is located, the white van turns into the neighborhood that borders the disc golf course. The one filled with people who seem to be against the disc golfers in the first place. It is a gated community surrounded by a stone wall that looks like it has been there a very long time, yet very well maintained.

"Well... this makes sense, sort of," Dina exclaims sarcastically.

The van keeps driving through the entire neighborhood until it comes up to a driveway with no house in sight. It's a long-wooded driveway with a metal locked gate out in front. The two of them park up the street and watch the van pull up to the driveway.

After a couple of seconds, the locked gate begins to open as the van sits there, waits for the gates to open enough to drive through, and then moves forward into the driveway. As soon as the van crosses the gate barrier, something happens. The van completely changes! It then goes from being a raggedy white van to a nice-looking black van as it entirely crosses the gate, making locating it impossible if they hadn't seen that.

"What the hell, did you just see that?" Glenn asks Dina.

"Yes, but I still don't believe it," Dina responds.

They watch the now black van disappear down the driveway and into the woods. The two jump out of the vehicle and run to the gate as fast as possible to get inside it before it closes.

"Made it!" Glenn says, panting, after running as fast as he could.

"Yeah, that was close," Dina responds, panting heavily. "Good thing we aren't in too bad shape, or else we wouldn't have made that."

They quickly gather their breath and continue down the driveway, hoping to see where the van ends up. After just a short little jog over the hill, they see the van pulling up to a log cabin-looking house. The driver steps out but does not look like the same driver they saw. The driver then turns into what appears to be a female, but that's not even the strangest part, for it doesn't look entirely human. He has dark eyes and a wrinkly face that would seem old yet appear young. Long hair, wearing a long dark jacket. Very sharp nails, almost claw-like. The being opens its mouth as if to shout out for someone, but at that moment, Glenn and Dina can see it has razor-sharp teeth.

"What the hell, this gets more and more weird!" Dina says, pointing out the obvious.

"Yeah, I feel like we entered the Twilight Zone or something. Did that person seriously turn into something not human?" Glenn responds back.

"I can't believe I'm about to say this, but yes, I think that person is a damn supernatural being of some sort," Dina says, struggling to believe what they just witnessed.

Hoping to get a better look at things, the two watch as the being enters the house, using the opportunity to get in closer. It appears to be a decent-sized home, most likely containing several rooms. Hoping that maybe their friends can be there, they look for a window to peek in to see if perhaps they can spot any sign of their friends inside. Locating a window, they peek in and see multiple beings cooking in a giant cauldron with something stewing inside it.

"Dude, seriously, are we being Punk'd?" Dina asks jokingly and out of curiosity. "This can't possibly be happening, this is the real world, crap like this doesn't happen."

"I know, right? I'm surprised it's not a candy house or something silly like that. Wait a minute, does that mean there may have been truth to some of those fairytales over the centuries? Ones talking about supernatural beings and witches that eat children like in Hansel and Gretel. This is so freaky!" Glenn responds.

Just then, they both turned around to find one of the beings standing directly behind them, then instantly in front of them. The being then blows mysterious powder at the two, and they immediately pass out, falling to the ground.

Chapter 10: Dungeons of Discs

Glenn starts to slowly come, too, "Where am I? What happened?"

Dina, lying next to him, also starts coming too. "I think those bastards came up behind us and did something to make us pass out."

They then hear a familiar voice, "Dina, Glenn, is that you two?"

"Holy crap, Amy? Is that really you?" Dina responds back.

"I'm here too," Mateo calls out, happy to hear his friends. "What are you two doing here?"

"We came looking for you, too; we saw the weirdest stuff, though. These people aren't normal," Glenn replies.

"Yeah, they're some sort of supernatural, form-changing, human-eating beings; it's like something out of a horror novel. They're fattening us up to eat us. We've already seen them take multiple people away since we've been here. And get this, everyone down here are all disc golfers, caught by that damn van," Amy responds.

"Hey, that's what we said too; it's literally like we are living in a Twilight Zone episode right now," Dina says, as they all start talking about everything that's been happening.

Realizing the dire situation the four of them are in, they begin to think about how to escape.

"I hate to say this, but maybe try telling them stories?" Dina suggests.

"What the hell, seriously? Like, are we acting like this is the Twilight Zone here?" Mateo asks.

"I suppose it's worth a shot; I mean, what else are we gonna do? Who knows what these "beings" are capable of?" Glenn responds back.

"Who's going to tell the stories then?" Amy then asks, weirded out by the whole situation.

The four of them, talking amongst themselves, figure out a plan of who will tell the stories. They unanimously suggest Glenn, and although Glenn argued that he can't tell stories very well, they all suggest that being such a movie freak he can handle it.

All he needs to do is think of his favorite movies and change them up a little while telling stories. Not having many options and fearing what they are dealing with, Glenn agrees to the outrageous plan, thinking there is no way in hell it can work, but at this point they need to try anything and everything they can think of.

Chapter 11: Tales for Survival

Now, the problem is when to launch the plan. They know they have to do it soon before they get too fattened up and can't run away to escape, for Mateo and Amy are already starting to show more weight. They agree to try the next time they come down to bring them food, which has been once a day, and they bring a day's worth of food for each person to eat all day.

The food is not ordinary either, Amy tried explaining to the group. You can't control yourself either; you eat the food that fattens you up more than you could imagine. Mateo, agreeing with her, reiterates their plan to try to escape as soon as possible and to try the stories.

After some time, three beings come down, bringing food for all. It's delicious looking, too, with turkey legs, perfectly cooked vegetables, all sorts of different types of beef and steaks, and all sorts of pies and cakes. It was a feast unlike anything they'd ever seen before, bigger than any Thanksgiving or holiday feast they'd had in the past.

"Eat up my lovelies," one of the beings tells everyone in the dungeon. Speaking with an old, crackly voice, exactly how you would imagine some old supernatural being would sound if they actually existed. Or, as they've just learned, they really have existed this whole time.

After the three witches are done serving food to everyone and are about to head back upstairs, Glenn tries to set their plan into motion.

Gathering up the courage to speak, Glenn then asks, "I was wondering if you three ladies would like to hear a story?"

"Oh, we like stories, don't we sisters? Please tell us one," they reply while huddling up to hear the story Glenn has in store for them.

Quickly, Glenn starts to tell a story: *The Disc Golf Lot*

"It was the start of the greatest summer of my life. I was getting ready to enter the 5th grade when I had just moved to town from out of state. That's the summer I met Benny. Little did I know he would get me out of the biggest pickle of our lives that summer.

It all started when I followed Benny to a hidden disc golf course in the middle of nowhere. If I knew what would have happened that summer, I maybe wouldn't have followed him that day.

The other kids were a rag-tag bunch, but to me, they were the greatest at disc golfing. I didn't know what I was doing at the time, I could only throw like 50 feet, but Benny would teach me everything I knew that summer about the sport of disc golf.

We would spend countless days on that disc golf course, where a house boarding the disc golf course had a mean dog that everyone feared. We didn't have many discs amongst us because we didn't have much money, so one day, when Benny threw a disc so hard that it flew apart, that's when all the trouble began.

Needing another disc for us to throw, I ran home to grab my stepdad's favorite collectible disc, but I had no idea how special and rare it was. To me, it was just another disc. I brought it back to the course for us to use, and because I was the hero with another disc, I was first up to throw. It ended up being the throw of a lifetime for me; the disc sailed and sailed, but unfortunately, it kept sailing into the fearsome dog's yard.

No one thought anything of it, for we'd thrown tons of discs into that yard that were never heard from again, but this wasn't just any disc; this disc was my stepdad's favorite and most prized possession. I then explained to the group that someone had signed it. I didn't know who it was, but it turned out that it was the most famous disc golfer ever.

This guy didn't have many signed discs out there. Making it even more valuable. The rest of the guys figured out the significance of the disc, and we started trying everything to get the disc back. We tried a rope and pulley system and a vacuum. I even pulled out every erector piece I had to try and get it, but we failed every time. It was wild. At one point, we went to the pool to see if we could figure out a new plan and to find our friend who would do anything to kiss the cute lifeguard on duty. In the end, he even married her and had children.

Another time, another group of disc golfers, the local rich kids, approached us and wanted to play against us in some team disc golf. We were not shying away from the challenge, and we totally accepted it. One of our friends even got in an argument with one of the other kids and totally won when he told him he threw like a 500-rated player when we were all 700 or above. We ended up playing the best disc golf we've ever played against those guys that day and took home the victory.

Well, anyway, back to the signed disc. No matter what we tried, we couldn't get the disc. So, one night, Benny had a dream, to wear the ultimate shoes, jump the fence and get the disc back himself. The next day, he attempted that very feat. Lacing up his slick new Converse, Benny prepared himself for the daunting task ahead.

After a running head start, he leaped the fence, grabbed the ball as quickly as possible, and jumped back over, safe and sound. Or so we thought.

The dog ended up jumping the fence to get Benny, so he had no choice but to book it out of there, and the dog pursued. It seemed like he ran all over town trying to lose that dog, you name it. Benny ran through it until he had the idea to run it back to its house.

When Benny got close, he again leaped the fence back into the yard, and the dog followed. However, the dog could not clear the fence this time, and it fell directly on the dog, pinning it down, letting everyone see that the dog was actually friendly; he wasn't trying to get Benny; he thought they were playing.

All of us ended up lifting the fence and freeing the dog. So, we knocked on the door to let the owner know the dog got out, and the fence fell. It turned out that the whole time, we could've just knocked on the door and asked for the disc back, and he would've got it for us, easy style. Go figure.

So, we explained to the dog's owner, a blind older man, what had happened, and another coincidence happened… it turned out not only did he have another signed disc by that disc golfer, but the disc had all his famous teammates' signatures on there too.

In the end, my stepdad got his original signed disc back, all chewed up and slobbered on, plus the new signed disc. I only got grounded for a month for it all, too."

"So, how did you like my story?" Glenn asks the ladies, hoping his parody rendition of one of his favorite movies passes as a good enough story.

Being entertained by his story, the beings want Glenn to tell them another one tomorrow upstairs while they cook. He agrees, for he feels this can be the next step in helping him and his friends escape this nightmare. The beings go back upstairs, leaving everyone once again in the dark, in the dungeon.

"Well, there's a start," Amy chimes in after the dungeon went dark. Knowing that gives them a little bit of hope that maybe they can somehow figure out how to escape.

"Everyone be prepared for anything tomorrow; if we see our shot to escape, let's take it," Dina adds.

After that, time felt like it took forever. None of the prisoners were able to have any idea whether it was dark or light out. They just had to lay there and wait until the beings brought them food again. Each one is lying in their cells, trying to sleep to make time go by faster, but they are unable to do so. I'm hoping they can somehow make it out the next day. Glenn is thinking away about what his next story is going to be.

Chapter 12: Chains Break

After hardly any sleep by any of the group, and what felt like an entire twenty-four hours gone by, the four of them anxiously await the beings to come and collect Glenn for their storytelling on the day, sitting silently in their cells, hoping for nothing but the best to be ahead. After what felt like several more hours had gone by, it appears the time is finally upon them.

The door to the dungeon opens, the lights come on, and only one being makes her way down to collect Glenn. They all got up with some pep in their step, for maybe this was their chance. With only one being, Glenn could possibly overpower her and get them all out. Waiting and seeing, they watched as the being slowly lagged her way up to Glenn's cell.

Then, something very unexpected happens. She blows the mysterious powder in Glenn's face and immediately knocks him out cold as he falls to the floor. She then drags him out of his cell, up the stairs, and into the main part of the house, leaving the dungeon door open. She returns a couple of seconds later, turns off the lights in the dungeon, and then closes the door behind her.

"Well damn," Mateo says after the door closes to the dungeon. "I was really hoping that was our chance."

"I agree," Amy says.

Now, all three of them can do is play the waiting game and hope it goes well for Glenn upstairs After a short time, Glenn is brought to the top floor of the house. When Glenn looks around and realizes he's upstairs already, he thinks, "Holy crap, now what are they up to?"

"Damn, I was hoping to take her out while she was alone," Glenn thinks to himself as he looks around and checks out the house. It looks like one would expect it to look, with how it looked on the outside, just a typical-looking house, minus the giant cast iron cauldron over a fire in a stone fireplace.

The kitchen, though, was a typical kitchen with normal-looking furniture, typical windows, and what looked like bedrooms. He also notices something of extra value for him and his friends: the front door is not locked!

"Well, now, there we go; if I can manage to get out and get everyone up here, we can get out the front door at least," Glenn thinks to himself as he's prepping to tell another story.

"The time has come for our story," the three beings tell Glenn as he's sitting in a cage as tall as the room in the dining room. The dining room is located just beside the kitchen, where the three beings cook up a feast. Glenn then sits down and prepares to tell them another story called *Major League Disc Golf.*

"Well, let me tell you three about the time I played team disc golf for a team called the Ohio Guardians. It all started when the team owner died, and his showgirl wife took over the team. She hated the team, so she hatched a plan to move the team to another state. However, she had to have the team perform incredibly badly to accomplish that goal. That's when she tried to put together the worst disc golf team known to man that no one has ever heard of. We came together at a minicamp to see if we could make the team. It was tough; we had to do weeks of drills and pre-season tournaments, and boy, were we awful. During the whole ordeal, we could be cut at any time, too, and no longer allowed on the team. So, several of us became

72

increasingly paranoid about it because, after all, it was only our lives. After a bunch of pre-season disc golfing, the final cut day was upon us.

Unfortunately, when I looked in my locker, I had a red cut tag in it. That's when I took it upon myself to yell at the manager. I told him that cutting me was the biggest mistake of his life and that every time I throw it against this team, I'm going to stick it where the sun doesn't shine. After my little rant and the manager just sitting there, staring at me blankly, he informed me that he hadn't cut me and that another disc golfer was playing a little prank on me. I knew just who it was, too. I stormed out of the office and attacked the other disc golfer because I was so angry.

So, our team was formed, and the season began, still expected to finish dead last by fans, critics, and the hopefulness of our team owner, for she still wanted to move the team. The season started out promising, for you know what they say: you can always tell how a season will go by the first hole, which was a birdie. However, we still weren't very good and just couldn't win. Oh yeah, some hilarious announcer who used to announce for the Milwaukee Brewers called our rounds. We also had another guy who could throw a mile, it seemed like, but man, you put him in the woods, and he couldn't throw at all.

Well, anyway, we kept losing and were dead last in the entire league, but that still wasn't enough for the owner. She wanted us to lose even more and by more significant margins. So, she took away things like our private jet for a crappy, scary plane and downgraded a lot of our equipment. One day, the manager called me into his office, ready to send me down to the minors of disc golf for my poor performances, but it turned out my eyesight just wasn't great. We ended up finding some sweet glasses that fit me, and I started doing much better.

Our team began to turn things around even. We started winning a few tournaments, and more fans began to show up to watch us compete. However, the owner started to get upset with us due to the winning, so she took our crappy plane and replaced it with a crappy bus to further downgrade us in hopes we would start losing again, but it didn't work.

One day, the team's general manager went and let the coach know what the plan was for the team the whole time. The

74

plan was all about how the owner was hoping we would lose cause she and everyone else thought so poorly of us as disc golfers. What she didn't see coming, though, was this motivated the hell out of us to win the whole damn thing. So, to motivate the team, we got a cardboard cut-out made of the owner, and every time we won a tournament, we peeled a section of her clothing off until she was fully revealed.

We started winning! Tournament after tournament, one after another, we were on fire. No one could stop us. Our teammates were nailing all their putts, getting aces, and crushing drives. Piece by piece, the clothing on the cut-out was coming off. We even started getting recognized and doing commercials; we even did a commercial for a company that takes a well-known credit card. We continued to win tournament after tournament, and we finally did it! We tied for first place in our disc golf division with the reigning champs.

There was one tournament left in the season, and sure enough, it was against the reigning champs. This left the winner of the tournament to be the winner of the division and earning a trip to the playoffs. Our team hadn't made the playoffs in a very long time, not for years and years, and we certainly hadn't won the division in decades.

Tournament day came, and the team was focused on getting the win. One player, our power thrower, who started doing better in the woods, wanted some extra power on the day, so he wanted to sacrifice a live chicken. However, we couldn't have the other teammates vomiting, so we got him a bucket of extra crispy chicken.

I wasn't slated to start the tournament, but at the last minute, the coach put me in to compete against the other team's most formidable player. We went back and forth all round, but in the end, my power off the tee was too much for him to handle, and I beat him, clinching us the win! We couldn't believe it. We beat the reigning division champs after rallying and coming back from behind.

The city was ecstatic. We finally brought them home the pennant for the first time in decades. We were local heroes. Everyone counted us out, and we still pulled it off!"

The beings, still cooking away, love the story! They were pleased with Glenn for the fascinating story, for they love their stories. Meanwhile, Glenn couldn't help but let out a big sigh of relief, for he was beyond thankful they didn't seem to watch TV and couldn't recognize his stories.

However, he was still left trying to figure out how to get out. After a short bit, two beings started bringing food into the dungeon, leaving just one upstairs with Glenn. The one being left upstairs begins to head towards Glenn's cage; she unlocks it and brings him out to take him downstairs. Only this time, she doesn't use the powder to knock Glenn out; she must've trusted him a little bit more due to the stories.

He quickly sees his opportunity, and with his tied-up hands, he puts them around the being's neck from behind and begins to strangle her Pulling with all his might as she struggles and fights to get free, gasping for air. After a couple of minutes of feeling her no longer move, he trusts that she is dead and begins to try and get himself free from the ropes tied around his hands.

Once free, he looks around for any type of weapon; looking through everything, he struggles to find anything, searching cabinet after cabinet, drawer after drawer, until he finally finds a knife drawer. He took a couple of knives out and headed towards the dungeon to free his friends.

The cabin was much bigger on the inside than it looked on the outside, which meant there were even more doors and rooms to check than initially planned. Not knowing which door was the door to the dungeon below, Glenn began opening door after door, going down a long hallway. He finally finds the dungeon door, the last door he checks.

Swinging the door open, Glenn quickly makes his way down into the dungeon. The light is not on, meaning the other two beings are not down there like he thought they would be. He quickly finds the light, turns it on, and heads down. With no hesitation, Glenn heads down the stairs and opens every single cell containing a fellow person. One by one, he lets everyone out.

"Head upstairs, down the long hallway, and you'll see the front door. Head to it and run away!" Glenn explains to everyone.

Next, he let out his friends; one by one, he led them out until everyone was free.

"Thank goodness you are alright!" Amy exclaims excitedly.

Then, all four of them give each other a giant hug as if it were a hug they never knew they would ever get to give again.

Chapter 13: A Nightmare Within

"We need to hurry; I don't know where the other two beings went," Glenn tells his friends.

The four of them begin heading upstairs and into the hallway, making their way towards the front door, but there is still no sign of the other two beings. They head outside without hesitation and keep running, not stopping for anything.

"Wait, where's everyone I let out before you all? With how big everyone's gotten, there's no way they could've gotten far. We should be able to see them," Glenn says, letting the group know his thoughts.

Not being able to waste time thinking about everyone else, they continue running towards the property's front gates. Just then, an alarm started to go off over intercoms in the area, but it was the sound of a car alarm, which puzzled the group, but they continue their way to the end of the property to get out, hoping, their van is still where they left it. They reach the end of the property, and sure enough, the gate is closed.

Using teamwork, they are able to get themselves over the wall, which is a six-foot stone wall that surrounds the entire property, just like the wall that surrounds the whole community. Once over, they still had to make it to their van. As they are walking, they notice the neighbors keep coming out of their houses and staring at them with the same sinister look the beings who captured them gave them.

"This is like something out of a nightmare," Mateo exclaims while they hurry to their van.

"The van is still there!" Dina says as she spots the van parked right where they left it.

As they get closer to their van, the people in the neighborhood slowly start walking further away from their front doors, almost to the street, still staring at them with those sinister grins. Even the kids of the families had the same looks.

"Is this whole neighborhood supernatural beings or something? How the hell have we never heard about this stuff being real?" Amy says quietly to the group, while she, at the same time, is beyond freaked out.

They reach the van and quickly get in and start it right up, but by this time, the van is surrounded by the people from the neighborhood. The neighborhood people begin banging on the van softly at first, but quickly, they start hitting harder and harder. Dozens of fists are pounding the van. Just then, the van's side and back windows broke open, and glass flew into their van, landing everywhere.

Glenn, Amy, Dina, and Mateo are beyond scared at this point, with nowhere to go; they are trapped in their van, feeling helpless. Then, the beings pull the doors open, dragging them all out into the street before they can even react. All the people from the neighborhood, one by one, started changing forms into their supernatural beings' forms, intensifying the living nightmare the four of them are currently living in. Then, a group of them drag Amy off and begin immediately eating her with no hesitation.

"AMY! NOOOOOOOOO!" Glenn yells out as he's watching these deranged beings eating his friend.

Just then, another group grabs Mateo, dragging him off a little way, and begins eating his body. Mateo screams in pain as these people start devouring his flesh and pulling his insides out while he's still alive. Making him see his own intestines ripping out of his body as he slowly dies with their hands shredding him to pieces.

Dina is now next, as they start ripping her apart, blood spraying everywhere as they do this right in the street. Glenn looks at the scene in sheer horror as he watches his friends being eaten alive.

Just then, the rest of the beings turn their sights on Glenn as they start to grab him and eat him, feeling their teeth ripping into his body. He can feel life slowly leaving his body as he lays there, helpless and dying.

THE END

Or So You Thought…

Chapter 14: Broken Sleep

Glenn quickly wakes up in a panic, checking his body, expecting to be eaten, but he's fully fine. "Holy crap, yes, I thought that was so real," he thinks to himself, looking around and realizing what must've happened. He woke up in a cell, in the dungeon, completely unharmed. However, it wasn't the same cell; it was one right next to the previous cell he was in, now placing him between Dina and Amy's cells.

"Glenn, are you alright?" Glenn can hear Amy's voice through the darkness of the dungeon.

"Yeah, I'm alright," he replies. "I had one of those dreams again, though."

"Wait, what dreams?" Dina asks.

What only Amy knew, and Dina and Mateo didn't, was that Glenn sometimes had dreams that came true. He saw the pandemic and various natural disasters and even saw Kyle Rudd, the newly crowned winner of Disc Golf Pro Worlds, who came out of nowhere to win it all. No one could have predicted that at all.

He explains to the group how he's had those dreams all his life, some big, some little. What he dreamt this time, though, was a must-know for the group.

"I have to tell you something; I'm pretty sure the whole neighborhood is in on this. So even if we escape from here, we must escape them too."

"What do you suggest we do then?" Mateo asks.

"We need to kill these beings so they can't trigger any type of alarm, and if we can manage to get off the property, we hope we can get to the van unnoticed and get the hell out of here," Glenn tells the group. "Hopefully, they will come to get me for another story today, and I promise you that if they do, we are getting out of here."

They go back to sitting in the quiet, waiting for their time. After a little bit, Amy quietly asks Glenn so no one can hear them, "What did you see in your dream?"

"You don't want to know," Glenn replies, "We can't get caught by the neighbors. The whole neighborhood is in on this. My best guess is the three holding us captive feed the whole neighborhood. And the food they cook are the people they hold captive, fattening us up with good food!"

"Oh my gosh!" Amy responds.

It goes back to complete silence after that, everyone with so much on their minds, all of them hoping that they will get out because they genuinely fear what Glenn saw in his dream.

After some more time, the dungeon door opens up, and the three beings holding them captive start heading down the stairs, hopefully coming down to Glenn. The three of them then walk up to another prisoner who's been down there with them, blow some powder in his face, knock him out, and drag him upstairs into the main part of the house.

Surprisingly, despite fattening the prisoners, one of the beings drags the body with such ease that it appears to weigh less than air, showing her strength, suggesting that these beings are most likely stronger than they appear at first sight, possibly making their efforts to escape much more difficult than the group initially anticipated. Throughout the day, they take prisoner after prisoner out, leaving the four friends puzzled as to what's going on.

"Are they cooking up all those people today? Are they maybe letting them go?" ask the four of them, growing more and more scared of the situation that they are in.

More time passes that same day, and the dungeon door opens back up; the lights come on, and only one is coming down this time. You can feel the anticipation in the air, the four of them hoping the witch is coming to get Glenn for a story and not to get one of them taken upstairs for who knows what. The being walks down the steps and walks straight up to Glenn's cell.

"We would like another story while we cook today," she turns and states.

She begins to reach for the powder that usually knocks everyone out, but Glenn suddenly reaches through the bars on his door; using his long, strong arms, he grabs her wrist to stop her. There's a struggle as she tries to fight Glenn's hand off the powder, but he manages to get a hold of the pouch she keeps it in.

Just then, the pouch pops open, and the mysterious powder goes up in the air. Glenn quickly jumps face down to the floor, holding his breath, to cover up and hopefully not be affected by the powder in the air.

"Glenn, are you out?" Amy says, curious if Glenn is knocked out from the powder as he lies still on the floor.

He begins to lift his head and replies, "I'm good. I'm up."

Once he rose to his feet, he saw what had happened. During the scuffle, he managed to pry the pouch open, and powder went up in the air, right into the witch's face, knocking her clean out. Glenn then reaches out for her body, pulling her fully close to him, wrapping his arms around her, while he starts searching her for the key.

"Here's the key!" he exclaims with joy. "Oh snap, check this out!"

He reaches back out, searching for the being some more, and pulls out a butcher's knife that she had on her. Glenn then unlocks his cell, gets out, and proceeds to unlock his friends' cells. By this time, Mateo and Amy have put on a significant amount of weight due to the feeding they've had to endure but are still confident they can get away.

Glenn then turns his sights on the knocked-out being on the floor. Equipped with the butcher's knife, he raises it high in the air and brings the blade down swiftly across her throat.

"What are you doing?" Amy gasps, not believing what she just saw Glenn do.

"I told you we have to kill them," Glenn responds, following another hack at her neck in an attempt to cut her head off.

Glenn then stops, leaving the being's head halfway on her body, blood pouring out everywhere. Glenn, also covered in blood at this point, holding the blade like something out of a horror movie.

"It had to be done. You don't want to know what these beings and the rest of their community will do to us." Glenn explains to the group. "We need to find the other two and kill them so they can't sound an alarm. Seeing how they just took the last prisoner not incredibly long ago, I bet they're preparing them all to cook them or are already cooking them all. We need to be super quiet but stay together as a group and look out for each other."

After grabbing the pouch of mysterious powder and Glenn equipped himself with the butcher's knife, the four quietly started going upstairs to the main part of the house. Reaching the top of the stairs, they slowly start creeping down the hallway, listening for the beings, trying to get an idea of where they can be. Although they are quite scared, they still have a sense of being the hunters at this point. Knowing what it's going to take to get out of the hellish situation they are in.

Slowly creeping down the hallway, they come to the kitchen, but no being in sight.

"Where the hell are they?" Dina asks.

"If you were preparing a human to be cooked, where would you take him?" Mateo also asks.

"Some sort of shed?" Amy suggests.

"Bingo!" Glenn, adding to the conversation.

The four of them make their way towards the front door and head out, hoping to find the beings out back. They begin to creep around the house, still trying not to make a sound, when they spot a shed out back. Still moving slowly as if being the hunters, they make their way to the shed and listen in, not hearing a single sound.

Glenn then makes some hand gestures, suggesting they look inside anyway. Dina prepares to open the door as Glenn raises the butcher's knife. She grabs the handle, then rips the door open! No one was inside, though, but what they did find was pretty horrific. It seems to be all the tools they use to prepare the bodies for cooking. However, some tools appear to be missing.

"They must still be in the house," Mateo suggests after seeing the missing tools.

"Crap, I think you're right. Weird how we didn't hear anything though when we were in there," Glenn responds. "We need to head back in to find them; if they find us gone, they will sound the alarm, and then we are screwed."

The four of them, still staying quiet, make their way back to the house to find the other two beings who held them captive. They reach the door and creep in, still listening carefully for any noises hinting at the whereabouts of any beings.

Creeping their way toward the kitchen first, the four of them start looking around for any weapons they can find. Dina finds another butcher's knife on a cutting board. At the same time, Mateo locates a heavy cast iron frying pan, and Amy finds a fire poker on the side of a fireplace that contains a giant iron cauldron.

Now equipped with a weapon, they make their way towards the long hallway with all the doors. Listening in on the outside of each door as they walk up to them one by one before opening up and checking inside. Door after door, they have no luck locating the beings. They come to the last door in the hallway before the dungeon door and start listening on the outside of it.

"Shh... you hear that?" Dina whispers.

"Yes, sounds like talking. They're in there!" Mateo whispers back.

Readying their weapons, they prepare to open the door and attack. Glenn holds his hand up with three fingers to count down.

3...

2...

1...

The group busts in, the other two beings are inside, startled by the intrusion. The group immediately rushes to attack them. One being, quickly grabbing for her pouch of mysterious powder, gets her wrist hacked at by Dina's butcher's knife. Mateo then hits her as hard as he can on the head with the cast iron pan. Blood pours from the being's head and wrist.

Glenn, at the same time, takes his butcher's knife and swipes at the other being, missing her. With the fire poker, Amy stabs the being right in the back. Regaining his composure after missing, Glenn then takes another swipe at the stabbed being, the butcher's knife sinking into her skull. She falls to the ground, instantly dead, her blood pouring from her body, covering the floor beneath.

Meanwhile, Dina and Mateo are repeatedly hacking at and hitting the other being, taking out their anger for being kidnapped by these sadistic things.

Breathing hard and covered with blood, the four of them stand there, trying to slow their breathing, for Glenn knows this is still far from over. They search around for anything to wipe the blood off and use a curtain covering a nearby window. Doing their best, they make it to the front door, hoping to reach the van that drove Glenn and Dina into the neighborhood. Trying to stay as calm as possible and act like nothing has happened, they make for the front gate. Upon reaching the gate, they find it locked.

"Wait, do you still have the dungeon cell key? Maybe that'll work." Dina asks Glenn.

Glenn then searches his pockets...

"Hell yeah, here it is!" He puts the key in the lock, and it turns! The lock releases, and then they unwrap the chain from the gate, making their way out onto the sidewalk. Walking towards the van, they try not to look around at all and look suspicious.

"So far, so good," Glenn lets the group know. "Let's keep it up, keep it casual, stay calm, and don't bring attention to us," he adds.

As they keep walking, they spot the van, where they parked it, and continue heading straight for it.

"Look!" Amy calls out.

A neighbor steps out of their house just as the group arrives at their van. Immediately giving them the same sinister look the beings have been giving them and the same one Glenn saw in his vision dream.

"Holy crap, what the hell is that?" Mateo asks as he starts to get even more frightened.

The group arrives at their van. Dina goes to the left tire on the back of the van and starts feeling around for her spare key.

"Got it, let's get the hell out of here," Dina exclaims, holding up the key to show everyone.

They all hop in immediately, but now more neighbors are outside their houses, just looking at them. All with the same sinister look, creeping the whole group out. Except for Glenn, who knows what can happen, he's trying to keep everyone as calm and focused as possible to make it out of the situation.

Dina starts up the van, throws it into gear, and takes off as fast as she can out of the neighborhood. Each house they pass has a family outside staring at them with same evil look, kids and all, just staring down at the humans as they attempt to escape.

As they approach the exit of the gated community, for there's only one way out, they notice a couple of cars trying to block the exit with more neighborhood people standing by them.

"Floor it, Dina, crash through the blockade, and get us the hell out of here," Amy says, scared to death that they will get trapped and caught.

Dina stomps on the gas pedal, accelerating the van. CRASH, as it hits the gap between the two cars, splitting them apart and the van making it through to safety.

"We made it!" Mateo, beyond happy, exclaims with a big sigh of relief.

Not slowing down, Dina drives as fast as she can to get as far away from the creepy community.

Chapter 15: Police Visit

"We need to go to the police," Glenn exclaims.

After they all agree, Dina starts making their way towards the police station. With the police station not too far away, they arrive after a short time. They head in to report what had just happened to them, hoping someone will believe them. As they are walking up to the counter, other police officers in the office, one by one, stop what they are doing and begin to look at the four of them. Being raggedy from being held captive for days sort of brought that attention.

"I don't have a good feeling about this," Dina exclaims, feeling all the eyes on them.

They reach the counter and begin to explain things. The officer working the desk directs them toward another police officer, who then takes their statements. After about an hour of the four of them telling them everything, the police officer instructs them to head home and stay safe, promising they will go check out the gated community and the house where they were held captive right away. So, the four of them head to Glenn's house for the night. They are too scared at this point to separate, power in numbers and all that.

Upon reaching Glenn's, not much is being said amongst the group, for they are in too much shock from what has happened to them. After setting up in the living room so they can all sleep in the same room, they all lay down for the night.

They still do not say much to each other, but they still make sure they have each other's back at the same time. The four of them, just lying there for hours, unable to sleep from being too scared, finally start dozing off one by one. Glenn is the last to fall asleep as he watches his friends, ensuring they are safe.

Amy quickly wakes up in a panic, breathing hard, sweat drenching her body from the nightmares she was having. She looks around, and sees Glenn's empty spot from where he was sleeping, blankets and everything still there.

Quietly calling out, "Glenn, Glenn" in a loud whisper type voice, seeing no signs of him, she proceeds to get up to locate him because something feels off to her. Slowly walking around the house, looking around, checking the bathroom, then the kitchen, but there's still no sign of Glenn anywhere.

Suddenly a light scuffle noise comes from the bedroom, Amy makes her way there. As she approaches the door, she can hear another strange noise coming from the bedroom, unable to make out what it is, she swings the door open.

What she saw next, nothing in life could ever prepare her for. For it was several people from the community eating away at Glenn. Amy can see his eyes, blank as can be, for he was already dead.

Blood everywhere, covering the walls, the bed, all over the beings eating at him. Just then Amy screams at the top of her lungs and runs back to the living room to wake her friends up to get out of there. As she arrives back at the living room, she finds more people from the community eating away at her two other friends.

Once again blood sprays everywhere, spreading across the floor, spraying the walls, puddling up beneath each of their bodies. Her friends are clearly already dead and there's nothing she can do, she feels so hopeless.

Amy then quickly grabs the keys for the van sitting on a nearby table, grabs them, then heads for the vehicle. Stumbling around, crying, scared for her life, she manages to get the van started and starts to back out of the driveway. Just then as she puts the van into drive and is about to take off, several of the sadistic beings emerge from the back of the van and attack her as if they were in there the whole time, waiting for her.

Immediately tearing into her flesh with their razor-sharp pointed teeth, while using their razor-sharp nails. Blood pours out of her and onto the van floor. Amy can feel life leaving her body.

She starts having flashbacks to all the good memories she had with her friends. All the time disc golfing, all the courses they got to play, all the good throws, all the great memories she had with her friends that she had had to watch being eaten. Until, nothing.

Chapter 16: A Sinister Call

Amy wakes up in a panic, scared out of her mind, breathing hard, and instantly crying.

"Are you okay?" Glenn asks as he, too, is woken up. Quickly consoling Amy, for he can tell instantly she must've had an insane nightmare. After all they've been through, especially her being kidnapped first, who wouldn't have nightmares?

He holds her as she just sobs in his arms. The other two friends are also waking up, each heading over to Amy to console her as well. The four of them are now sitting in a giant group hug in the middle of the living room, comforting their scared friend.

"I had the worst nightmare," Amy tells the group. "The rest of the beings found us here and ate you three. I got in the van to drive away, but as I was, I, too, was killed. It was horrible and felt so real."

All four of them were sitting, all still hugging Amy, trying to calm her down from her horrible nightmare. No one was surprised considering what they all had gone through, for they, too, each were having nightmares themselves, just not at the same level.

It is still dark out, so they all intend to go back to sleep. However, Amy is unable to do so under the circumstances. Since she is unable to, Glenn decides to stay up with her to comfort her. The two get to talking and start reminiscing about all the good times they used to have with Glenn's little brother. Then they start wondering if maybe the beings had anything to do with his disappearance.

A body was never found, and the way he disappeared was pretty mysterious, they discuss. Although his little brother was long ruled dead, it still never sat right with Glenn or Amy. Seeing how sneaky these beings seem to operate, it's not a far-off concept that they could have had something to do with his disappearance.

After talking for hours, Glenn and Amy are still awake when the sun starts rising. Mateo and Dina were now waking up for the day with them. Talking and waking up, the group decides it's breakfast time, and Mateo offers to cook them a feast while they wait for the police to call.

"What's everyone want?" Mateo asks, prepared to cook whatever the group wants.

"Oh, how about those yummy breakfast sandwiches you make?" Dina responds.

Agreeing, Mateo starts to cook up their breakfast. First, he pulls out some bacon, separates it, lays it in the pan, and starts frying it up. Slicing up some bagels, toasting them, buttering them, then putting them aside, Mateo waits for the bacon to finish cooking. After a little bit, the bacon is cooked just how they like it, and it's time for Mateo to fry some eggs. One by one, he fries up the eggs, loads them on the bagels with bacon, and puts a slice of cheese on each.

"Foods done," he calls out to everyone.

They all eat up and, as always, love Mateo's cooking. He's always been the group's cook cause, after all, every group's got one. Not much time passes until Glenn's phone starts ringing. He picks up his phone to see who's calling, and seeing it's the police, he gets a little excited and hopeful when answering the phone. Quickly, his hopeful expression turns to disgust, and after a short bit, he hangs up the phone. He explains to the group what the cops told him on the phone.

"They said they found nothing. They went to the house and found three ladies living there, all acting sweet and innocent. They searched the outside of the property and found nothing. I interviewed the neighbors and found nothing suspicious. The group immediately feels disgusted and disappointed with the police.

"What do they think we did? Did we make it all up? So what now?" Dina asks.

"I don't know. We can either go about our lives and pretend nothing happened or go back and do something about it," Glenn explains to the group.

The group, scared to death of what can happen to them, chooses not to go back to the community and do anything about it, hoping everything can be forgotten over time, hoping just to go back to their everyday lives as if nothing had ever happened, very disappointed that nothing can be done. They go to their own homes, not knowing what else to do.

That evening, while sitting at home, watching TV, Amy's phone starts to ring with a local number. Not used to seeing local numbers calling her, she decides to answer it because it's usually just spam or bill collectors.

"Hello?" as she picks up the phone.

However, there's no noise, just silence.

"Hello?" she asks again.

Then, out of nowhere, she can hear the faint noise of someone breathing. Amy immediately hangs up her phone, scared more now than ever.

Chapter 17: Blood Oath

As soon as everyone leaves, Glenn turns on his TV to help distract his mind from the horrors that have happened. After all, they killed three people, and although maybe not fully human, the four of them still killed them. They were kidnapped and held captive, along with whatever happened to them at that house that made them want to eat all that food.

Moment after moment, everything that occurred at that house, replaying in Glenn's head. That's when Glenn decides to start cleaning. Hour after hour, he spends cleaning. Frantically cleaning everything: the bedroom, living room, bathroom, kitchen, even cleaning his toilet, oven, you name it, everything was getting a cleaning to take his mind off of the sheer horror of things. It is into the evening by this time, and Glenn is still cleaning. Just as he is finishing up, his phone rings. He picks it up and sees that Amy is calling, so he answers.

"What's up Amy, are you okay?" he asks.

"I just had a strange phone call; when I answered the phone, it was silent at first, and then I could hear the faint noise of someone breathing. So, I hung up and immediately called you." Amy responds to Glenn.

After the two chat back and forth for a bit, Glenn invites Amy to return to his house. She agrees and tells him that she will head straight over, for she doesn't want to be at home alone anymore.

Around fifteen minutes later, Amy comes walking into Glenn's house. They've all been friends for so long that none of them knock when they go to each other's houses. Glenn ends up pouring them both a glass of wine, and they sit down and start talking. They end up talking and talking, drinking glass after glass of wine until the whole bottle is gone.

Before they both knew it, they were kissing. They've never kissed each other before but have both liked each other for a long time now. It is instantly passionate, like it was always meant to be. One thing led to another, and the next thing they knew, they were in the bedroom having sex.

"I have a confession to make. I've loved you for a long time now." Amy says, admitting her feelings for Glenn.

"I have felt the same way," Glenn responds.

The two continue, deep into the night. A moment they've both been longing for so long now. When they are done, they cuddle up and fall asleep, holding each other in their arms.

Chapter 18: Hunt for Vengeance

One Week Later

"Hey Amy, have you seen my disc golf bag?" Glenn yells out as he's searching around for his disc golf bag.

Today is the first day the group is heading out disc golfing since the whole incident occurred. Amy has been staying with Glenn this week ever since they slept together. They are officially a couple at this point and are practically living together since it feels so natural.

Amy, also gathering up her disc golf bag, shouts back to Glenn, "I haven't seen it; I'll help look after I gather my stuff up, though."

She gathers up her stuff, fully ready to head out, and then proceeds to help Glenn find his bag. It doesn't take long before they find it, making them fully prepared to go. Seeing what happened near the other disc golf course and that part of town, the group decides to check out a course on the other side of town, another heavily wooded course on the city's outskirts.

They head out intending to meet up with Mateo and Dina at the course on hole one. Since the course is on the opposite side of town, it takes them a little longer to get there. They pull in, and sure enough, Dina and Mateo are already there, waiting for them, throwing some warm-up putts. Glenn and Amy park, hurry up, and get their stuff out, for they are eager to disc golf again. Hoping it would take their mind off of things and relax a little bit. After all, the best therapy is a round with your friends.

Throughout the round, the four of them laugh and have a great time, as if nothing has ever happened, which is precisely what they hope to get out of throwing a round. They're throwing great, too, with birdies left and right, killer drives off the tee, all while nailing their approach shots. They all have killer rounds out there, along with the time of their lives.

As they finish up the eighteenth and final hole, they start discussing what they will do that night, finally agreeing to hang out at the bar and have a few drinks. They putt out on the final hole and head to their vehicles to head out and that's when Dina notices something. She starts heading towards the park bulletin board. Most disc golf courses tend to have bulletin boards to post about various events and such. She rips something off it and brings it to the group, now huddled up, curious about what Dina is doing. It's a missing person's poster of a disc golfer.

"Do you think it was those people?" Dina asks the group, hating having to bring anything up on that subject.

"Very well could be. They clearly had a thing for disc golfers," Amy answers back.

After talking back and forth for a bit, the group decides that there's nothing they can do. That, even if it was them, what can the four of them do? They're not professional killers but ordinary people who love disc golfing.

They end up hopping in their cars to meet up at the bar to have a couple of drinks. Getting ready to pull out of the parking lot, Amy notices something nearby that catches her attention. It was the white van that abducted her!

"Drive by it, Glenn?" she asks.

"I don't think it's a good idea," he repeats, wanting to just get out of there.

Amy then starts signaling out of her window towards Dina and Mateo, pointing out the van to them. She can tell they see it but are awaiting some signal from Glenn and Amy's vehicle on whether to drive over to it. Amy then pleads with Glenn to check it out, insisting that maybe they can help someone not be kidnapped or, at the very least, put a stop to it. Or, at least for now, make sure they don't kidnap someone else today.

Glenn agrees and signals to the group that they are going to sit back and watch to make sure they don't get anyone. They watch for hours as the van just sits there, the door open with the discs exposed, but not a single person walks up to it. Until the driver finally gets out, closes up the van, and starts to head out.

The van takes off in their direction, and right as it drives by, the driver turns and gives Amy and Glenn that same sinister look. As if letting them know, "I know you were watching, so are we." Sending chills down both their spines.

With nothing they can do because they know where that van is from anyway, the crew heads to the bar to meet up for their drinks. While there, they start talking about what they can maybe do about the community of supernatural beings in their town. They discuss just packing up and getting out, trying again with the police, and maybe telling them more about the van this time, or perhaps just trying to take them out themselves. Discussing it for hours while having a few drinks each, but unable to come up with something on the spot, they decide to head home for the night to think about things.

That night, all four of them think hard about what they can do about this whole situation since the police can't seem to do anything. Not wanting to live in fear, but they aren't killers either. So, really what can they possibly do?

Amy and Gleen, who are still staying together, decide to watch a movie, Major League, which happens to be Glenn's favorite movie; who would've guessed it?

About halfway through the movie, they hear a loud noise outside. Curious about the noise, Glenn gets up and goes to the window to check it out. It is the white van in his driveway! Freaking out, he lets Amy know right away that the van is at the house. They both quickly arm themselves with the closest weapons they can find. Amy locates a heavy little statue on a couch end table while Glenn heads into the kitchen to grab his chef's knife, the only real knife in the house. Standing back at the window, they peek out through the blinds with curiosity but see nothing except the white van.

"Wait here; I'm going to go check it out," Glenn tells Amy.

Glenn proceeds to head outside to investigate. He slowly starts walking up to the van, looking all around in the process but seeing nothing, not even seeing a driver in the driver's seat. As he steps even closer, the van's side doors open up. Glenn steps back in anticipation of anything bad that can happen.

Suddenly, two objects come flying out at him; he jumps back, not knowing what they are. They roll up to his feet. He looks down in complete horror as he sees it's the heads of Dina and Mateo, their heads looking as if they have been chewed off of their bodies. Their eyes rolled back in their heads. Glenn can hear Amy scream from the house as she realizes what is thrown at him. Heading back into the house, Glenn closes and locks the door behind him, grabs Amy, and heads for the back door.

Both in complete panic scared out of their minds, and heartbroken over the death of their best friends, they leave through the back door and start running. They find an alley and continue running, trying to stay out of sight. Unexpectedly, a car comes out of nowhere and turns onto the ally they are on.

Fearful that it's the bad creatures, they continue running. The car speeds up as it spots them. Then the worst thing that could happen happened. Another car pulls up, blocking the end of the alley that they are in; with the other car coming up on them fast, with nothing left to do, they throw up their hands in defeat. People then start coming out of every door to both vehicles and look at them with those sinister looks.

One of them, who appears to be the leader, sniffs the air. "That is a familiar scent." Still in his normal-looking human form, he sniffs the air again and points at Glenn, "I've tasted one with blood like yours before."

Glenn's thoughts immediately turn to his missing brother, always knowing that he never drowned and that someone took him. Pissed off, he begins to yell at the being, screaming and cussing, trying to hold back his anger. He lunges at the being, and they begin to fight. Punching and kicking, and then slamming the being on the pavement, hurting him. The being then calls out for a group to attack Glenn and another to get Amy.

Glenn then turns to Amy and yells, "RUN!"

She starts running, sliding over the hood of the car blocking the alley, Glenn right behind her. Two beings shed off from the rest of the group to get the vehicles while the rest take off on foot to chase down Glenn and Amy.

"We're not going to die; we're going to get away and get revenge for Dina and Mateo, I promise you," Glenn lets Amy know as they are both running for their lives.

The beings, not fully human, appear to be faster than Glenn and Amy, so they begin to do what they can to escape. They climb fences, go through yards, and throw stuff in their path, anything to slow down their pursuers. It feels like they've been running forever as they both begin to get tired.

They can hear the cars driving on the nearby streets, the chasers gaining on them with every second. Right as they thought they were about to be caught, they ran into a yard with some garden tools. Amy picks up a shovel as fast as she can and swings it wildly in the air. Smacking dead across the side of the head of one of the beings, knocking her down, blood pouring out of her head and drenching her hair. Blood puddles beneath her dead body.

Glenn sees a metal rake and picks it up. He swings it wildly in the air, the rake spikes catching another being on the side of their body. The spikes digging in, the rake sticking into the person as blood starts to run down the handle and drip on the ground.

Amy then picks up a garden hoe, swings it, misses, but backs a couple of them up. She swings again as one tries to get her. She sticks the hoe right into the stomach of the being. The being yells out in pain as the hoe is ripped out of him, tearing flesh from his body. Blood shooting out and spraying Amy, splattering across her clothes and face.

Glenn then grabs another and starts wrestling with him, slamming him to the ground. He then stomps the being's head repeatedly until blood starts pouring out. A being then grabs Glenn, throwing him to the ground. Amy, now covered in blood, swings the hoe around, fighting for her life, and is finally grabbed from behind.

Glenn starts getting raging mad, "LET HER GO!" as he runs and grabs the being off Amy, tossing him to the ground. Amy also falls to the ground in the exchange. Jumping on top of the being he just pulled off Amy, Glenn hits him in the face. Repeatedly slamming his fists into the being, his knuckles turn bloody and still he continues beating the being, doing it for his dead friends. Glenn then gets up and turns to Amy to help her, but he's too late. They are on Amy eating her alive. Amy is reaching out for Glenn with the last of her strength.

Glenn then leaps at them, trying to knock them off of her. He's suddenly pulled back and thrown to the ground by the two beings that were in the cars. Who made their way there during all the fighting. The two then jump on Glenn and begin beating him. Kicking him on his body, his face, Glenn coughing up blood as they do so. Then they begin to eat him alive; having no strength left, he's unable to fight back as their teeth tear the flesh from his body. Pulling his intestines from his body as he lies there, barely alive, still able to feel everything, wishing for a quick death. Then, he takes one last breath as he dies, lying in a puddle of his own blood.

Chapter 19: House of Horrors

Glenn wakes up suddenly; Amy sound asleep next to him. Glenn, pouring sweat, starts shaking Amy in an attempt to wake her.

She wakes up groggy, asking Glenn, "What's wrong?"

He then explains to her that he had another dream, one where he feels it will come true. "They know where we all are, Mateo, Dina, and us, and they're coming!" He tells Amy in panic, fearing he may lose his friends.

It is early morning; by this time, the sun is just barely starting to rise. The two pick up their phones, and each one begins to call a friend. Glenn tries to call Mateo, while Amy tries to call Dina. Neither one got an answer. Scared for the worse, the two dress as quickly as possible to drive to check on their friends. They head to the car, start it up, and decide to head to Dina's first. With Glenn driving, Amy sits in the passenger seat, calling Mateo and Dina nonstop, but there is still no answer.

They arrive at Dina's and rush in. The front door is locked, but they know where she keeps her spare. Searching the top of the nearby windowsill and finding the key, Amy unlocks the door, and they both head in.

"Dina, Dina, where are you? Are you here?" Amy calls out frantically. She then searches the bedroom while Glenn searches the rest of her house. To her surprise, Amy finds Dina in her bed, sound asleep and unharmed. Startled by the noise and the fact someone is in her home, Dina wakes up suddenly.

"What the hell is going on? What are you two doing here?" Dina asks.

Glenn, hearing the talking, heads to the bedroom. "I had a dream; they know where you live and are coming for you," Glenn informs Dina. "We were worried about you. We tried to call, but there was no answer."

"Well, of course, I didn't answer. It was the crack of dawn, and I was sleeping. I don't sleep with the ringer on," Dina tells them. She then shoots out of bed, completely panicked, "What about Mateo? Is he alright and safe?"

Glenn informs her they came here to check on her first and were heading to Mateo's next and to meet them there. Dina agrees, letting them know she will get ready immediately and head over there. Glenn and Amy then run to the car to go to Mateo's next to check on him. While heading there and with Glenn driving, Amy again keeps calling Mateo but has no luck reaching him.

With Mateo not living too far from Dina, they arrive there in no time and run up to the door; of course, it's locked. Not having a spare key, they run around the house to Mateo's window and look in. He's lying there motionless. They then begin to frantically knock on the window, scared for the worse.

Mateo starts to move, turning over and looking right at them at the window. Beyond puzzled, he gets up out of bed and shrugs his shoulders as if saying, "What the hell are you doing here." Signaling Glenn and Amy to head to the front door, Mateo heads there to let them in.

"What's going on, guys? I was sleeping," Mateo asks, yawning and groggy from being woken up weirdly. Glenn and Amy walk into his house, and Mateo closes the door behind them.

Glenn informs him that he had a dream, that the beings were coming for all of them, and that the beings know where they all are. He also lets Mateo know that they have already stopped by Dina's and that she's okay. She was just getting dressed and then meeting up with them here.

While they wait for Dina to arrive, Mateo makes a fresh pot of coffee for the bunch. It finishes, and he pours their cups. They then proceed to wait and talk in the living room. Anticipating Dina's arrival at any point. The only problem is that time keeps going by, and no Dina.

Chapter 20: Slaughter in the Shadows

Realizing how much time had passed and that Dina should have been there by now, they began to call her. Now that she's awake and knows what's happening, they feel she should answer her phone immediately. Only, no answer.

They call again and again with no answer. The group begins to panic and agrees to head over to Dina's as a group in Glenn's car to check on her. It doesn't take long to arrive at Dina's, especially with how fast Glenn drove, and they run straight into her house. The door unlocked and all. They start looking all over and calling out for her, but there is no response.

Mateo heads to the bedroom to check there. Suddenly, they heard a loud yell throughout the house. It was Mateo, yelling outside Dina's door; their worst nightmare had come true. Dina's lying there on the bed, what remains of her, that is. Clearly, she had been eaten by several of those sadistic beings, the blood still fresh and dripping off of the sheets. Pieces of flesh and bones lay everywhere throughout the room, blood splattering on every surface, her scalp with her hair still attached lying amongst her clothes.

Amy then comes running up to the room, screaming in horror at the sight of her best friend. Glenn comes up and hugs her, turning her head away from the bloodbath horror in the room. Glenn does not believe what is happening, hoping he will wake up, but knowing this time, it's actually for real. Their friend is now dead, leaving the three of them to figure this out.

With tears streaming down her face leaving streaks of mascara like war paint, Amy pulls herself from Glenn's shoulder, "Let's kill them, kill them all!"

The group, in 100% agreement, quickly starts to turn their sorrow into anger, knowing fully well what has to be done at this point. They now begin to work on their plan. With none of them having any experience with guns, they agree to head over to the nearby hunting/sporting goods store to look at things like axes, knives, and bows, especially a bow with Amy's archery background.

It's only a short drive away, so they load up in Glenn's car and head over there right away, wasting no time. All they can think of is getting revenge for their friend Dina. Arriving at the store, they park and head in. As they walk into the entrance, something on the wall grabs Glenn's attention; he then walks up to it and pulls it off the wall.

"What is it?" Amy asks.

"It's that guy Jonah we met before all hell broke loose. He was that guy that saw my sweet shot at the course next to the community," Glenn explains to Amy and Mateo as he shows them the missing person's poster on the wall.

Now even more angry at the disappearance of another disc golfer, the crew heads into the store to check things out. While the group is there checking out everything, they start imagining how they'd like to kill those sadistic bastards. Thinking about how sweet it would be to get revenge for their fallen friend and the nightmare those beings put them through before that.

Glenn heads over to the hand axes, swinging each one, seeing which one has better balance and feel in his hands, then picking out one he likes. Amy, having done archery as a kid and teenager and being quite good at it, was checking out all the bows. Finding one that reminded her of her old one, for it had been a few years since firing a bow. She feels instantly comfortable with the bows in her arms and finds the perfect one for her.

Meanwhile, Mateo had something else on his mind. He was checking out the baseball bats, for he used to be a baseball player in high school. Thinking of making a makeshift weapon for his supernatural being killing tool. Finally, finding the perfect bat for him, he grabs some nails to hammer into it to make himself a spiked bat. Now, with their weapons of choice, the crew proceeds to the checkout.

Just imagine something out of a Suicide Squad movie, the three of them walking in slow-mo, music playing in the background, as they push their shopping cart that contains their supernatural being killing items. They check out, but while receiving the strangest looks from the cashier.

"Are you guys going to go kill zombies or something?" The cashier jokingly asks the three of them.

Laughing, one says, "No, but something similar."

As they try to brush off the almost accurate joke of the cashier, for little did the cashier know that the three of them were going to be doing some serious hunting. Something the three of them never thought would ever happen in life, for none of them had that on their bingo card.

After checking out, they head to the car, pack up their stuff, and then head to Glenn's father's house, fearing that the beings will find them at one of their houses. Glenn rarely goes home these days since the disappearance of his brother all those years ago, for it brought back far too many painful memories. He always blamed himself for that day and his brother's disappearance.

Especially now after his vision dream of them saying they knew his brother, suggesting they had something to do with his disappearance, most likely eating him as well. It's bringing everything back again, getting him increasingly angry and wanting answers.

Upon arriving at Glenn's father's house, they are instantly greeted with open arms, but that soon changes when the crew tells him why they are there. Glenn starts explaining everything to his father, from everyone being kidnapped to Dina being killed that morning, and about the possibility of what happened to Garrett and these beings being responsible for him.

However, Glenn's father did not take all this well, not well at all. His father, having mixed feelings about everything, led off with the suggestion that there was no way these people had anything to do with Garrett's drowning. His father still believes to this day that Garrett drowned since the police said so, even though a body was never found. Then, they suggest they call the police instead and let the police handle it. He talked with Glenn for a long time, slowly calming him down.

After a while, Glenn agrees to give the police another try. This time, they call the police and advise them to check Dina's house and that they'll find her body there. They'll be able to tell right away that she was eaten alive, adding proof to the original story they told the police.

Glenn then calls and tells them everything. The police then inform him that they'll check Dina's house immediately and call him back. About 40 minutes go by until the police call back. Glenn answers the phone, hoping for some good news that the police will finally believe their original story so maybe they can get some actual help.

However, Glenn's face quickly turns to a "what the hell" look as he listens to what the police have to say. He's not on the phone long before hanging up. He stands silent at first, holding his head down, shaking it back and forth, not believing what he was just told.

Amy then asks, "What is it? What did they say?

"You're not going to believe this. They found nothing, no body, no blood, no signs of struggle; her car was gone, and a bag looked like it was packed. They said they think she just up and left town," Glenn answers.

"That's complete bull," Mateo responds, "We saw the body; blood was everywhere. How can that be covered up so quickly?"

The group, beyond puzzled at this point, for they have no idea what they are entirely dealing with, decide to return to their original plan of killing them all. They begin to prepare themselves and their weapons for the upcoming slaughter, hoping to bring down those sadistic beings. Glenn's father has a workshop, so Glenn begins to sharpen his newly bought hand axe.

Meanwhile, Mateo is pounding nails into his bat to make it a lethal, being killing weapon. Amy, outback, was brushing up her archery skills. Getting back into her old habit and hobby she once loved. They spend all day preparing for the bloodbath that lies ahead. Once night comes, they retire to the main house and hang out with Glenn's father, eating dinner, having some dessert, and having some drinks, trying to have a good time, knowing that it could very well be their last.

After what felt like hours of just sitting around and talking, they all head to bed. Mateo, Amy, and Glenn are all set up in the living room, spreading out their sleeping bags and lying close together. Hoping this is not the last night they ever get to spend with each other. That night, the three of them lay there in silence, staring up at the ceiling, struggling to fall asleep, hoping they make it through the day tomorrow. None of them want to die but fear that if they don't strike, these beings will surely get them and kill them all. These beings don't seem willing to leave loose ends and all three of them know they are loose ends.

As Mateo lies there, he finally falls asleep and enters a dream state. Instead of a dream, though, he experiences a hellish nightmare. Reliving that moment, when he saw his friend's body, dead on her bed, with blood all over the room, covering what was left of her body. Only this time, Amy and Glenn are not there with him. He's just alone, staring in horror at his dead friend, then her eyes open up.

Mateo jumps back in fear at the startlement, except he leaps back into something soft. He feels behind him, feels like clothing. He quickly turns around and stumbles backward, right onto Dina's dead body. It's the beings in their supernatural form, their mouths open as they walk toward Mateo as if they are going to eat him.

He tries to get up to get away, but he can't. No matter what he tries, he can't seem to stop slipping into the blood. He struggles and struggles to get away but just can't until the beings are entirely upon him. Standing over him, mouths still wide open. He can see their razor-sharp teeth. They then begin to eat him alive, Mateo screaming, still slipping around in the blood, trying to get away as they eat his flesh from his bones.

He then wakes up! Sitting up quickly, panting incredibly hard, sweat covering his entire body, drenching his clothes and sleeping bag. Pulling open his sleeping bag to air out, he lies down and stares back at the ceiling for a few seconds before checking on his friends. Both Amy and Glenn, still lying in their sleeping bags, sound asleep. After laying there for hours, the sun finally comes up, and Mateo is still just staring up at the ceiling, waiting for everyone to wake up. Which they finally do about an hour later. The three of them are just lying there silent, scared, yet determined to make it through the day ahead.

Chapter 21: The Stone Fortress

To start the day, Glenn's dad decides to cook the crew a wonderful breakfast. Cooking up eggs, sausage, bacon, bagels, and hash browns is a true feast and a wonderful, possibly last, breakfast. They eat silently, still focusing on the day ahead: Glenn's dad is sad. Not fully believing but knowing that his son and his friends may be heading off to do something stupid. Also, knowing that his son is his own man and that if this is a fight that he feels he needs to do, then he's going to let him.

Once they finish breakfast, the group begins to plan for how they're going to go about killing the beings. After discussing several plans, they agreed to go house to house as quietly as possible. Waiting until dark to put their plan into action.

As nightfall approaches, they load up in Glenn's father's vehicle to head to the gated community that housed these beings, hoping to cut back on being recognized and setting off any type of alarm. Approaching the community, they decide to park a little way away to help remain undetected, helping provide some sort of surprise to their attack.

They park, hop out, and slowly make their way towards the walls that surround the community. Like the beings' house where they were held captive, the whole community had a stone wall, as if it had been there for a couple hundred years. Although the gate to the community is open, they try to be stealthier by jumping over the wall directly behind the first house they intend to start at.

Using teamwork, the three scale the wall and start walking slowly and quietly toward the first house. They spot a back door and try it out; it opens! Walking in, staying as quietly as possible, they start creeping into the house. A light is on in a room they can see, so they head there to check it out. They walk in on a normal-looking family, just sitting there while eating dinner. Glenn, Amy, and Mateo's weapons are all raised as if ready to strike anything that moves. With puzzled looks on their faces, they slowly lower their weapons.

The dad starts to speak, "May I help you?"

"Um, I think we are in the wrong house," Glenn responds, apologizing for interrupting their dinner.

The family is very polite, especially considering the circumstances of the three of them breaking in, acting like they're prepared for the zombie apocalypse. While approaching the back door, getting ready to head out and be on their way, Glenn hears something coming from the family in the dining room, so he stops listening more carefully.

"Don't do it," someone says softly from the family, but being around the corner, they couldn't tell who. Suddenly, the little boy from the family walks around the corner and gives them the same sinister look that so many have before. Then, right before their very eyes, they transform into one of the beings and start running directly at the trio. Panicked and completely caught off guard, they stood there, frozen. The little boy, who turned into a being then jumps at them as if flying, then bam! He drops to the floor with Glenn's axe stuck in his head. Glenn scores a perfect shot, giving a little fist pump, then ripping his axe from the little being's skull, readying for the next kill.

The three looked at each other as if to say, "It's going time," and then charged in on the rest of the family. By the time they return to the dining room, the rest of the family, a father, mother, and another child, a daughter, are all in their supernatural forms. However, that did not stop Mateo, Glenn, and Amy from charging in with determination and swinging, wanting revenge for their fallen friend.

Mateo takes his bat and charges the father first, swinging as hard as possible, trying to hit him. The father, reaching for a pouch, most likely of the mysterious knockout powder, is struck by Mateo with his spiked bat. Hitting the being right in the stomach. Mateo quickly pulls the spiked bat out of the being, gutting him in the process. Intestines start pouring out on the floor, along with more blood than you could imagine.

At the same time, Amy is in the doorway, shooting arrows, one into the head of the father, who's already dead, but like they say, rule #2 is to double tap. She then sets her sights on the mother, missing her first shot but reloading quickly, firing off another arrow, shooting her right in the eye.

Next comes the other child, who at this time seems to be the strongest, for she has Glenn down on the ground, trying to kill him. Unable to fight back, he calls out for help. Amy then fires the arrow at the supernatural child, hitting her right in the back, not slowing her down. The supernatural child is still attacking Glenn, clawing and biting, covering him with deep scratches.

Mateo walks up and swings with all his might, WHAM, hitting the being with all his might right on the side of her head, knocking her head clean off her body. Blood starts shooting out of her neck, covering Glenn while he lies beneath her headless body. Quickly throwing off the headless corpse, Glenn gets to his feet, wide-eyed, completely covered in blood. The three look at each other blankly now that the battle is over and won. Glenn is overcome by all the blood covering his entire body and nearly faints.

Chapter 22: Dreams of Dina

"Wow, did that just seriously happen? Amy asks, stunned about all the deaths that just occurred, not believing how powerful the little girl was, being able to take an arrow like it was nothing. As they continue onward, hoping they don't run into even stronger ones along their journey of bringing mayhem to these things.

Heading to the kitchen to look for some liquids, they stumble upon something: human body parts in their kitchen, along with a human head. Looking at the head with a puzzled look, Glenn recognizes who it is. It's Jonah!

The disc golfer he met and whom they saw on a missing person poster at the store where they got their weapons from. Confirming to the group how much good they are doing by doing this. How many lives they may be saving by stopping these sadistic beings who kidnap, kill, and eat people?

They clean up, check Glenn's wounds, which appear to be okay, and prepare to head to the next house over. Hopefully, they are not making enough noise to raise any type of alarm or hint that they are coming for them all After rehydrating by raiding the fridge, the three set off to the next house.

Going back out the back door and staying in the backyards, they begin to creep as they get outside. Once again, they are trying to remain as quiet as they can. Creeping closer and closer to the next house, no fence or anything was separating the two, making the journey a little easier for them.

Upon arriving, they again plan to go in through the back door since it worked well last time. They reach the back door and check to see if it's unlocked. It is! Quietly opening the door all the way and stepping inside, leaving the door partially open to not make more noise by closing it, they find themselves in a mudroom, with another door to the house directly in front of them.

Mateo begins to slowly open the door, and the three of them peek in, immediately coming face to face with an adult woman carrying a laundry basket. The woman drops the basket and instantly transforms into a being, catching Glenn and Mateo off guard. Suddenly, they feel something go right between their heads as an arrow enters the being's head, directly on her forehead.

"Holy moly, sweet shot," Glenn informs Amy in a whisper voice.

Fearing they made too much noise, they stood there for a minute listening to hear if anyone had heard them and to any signs of someone sneaking up on them. After a short bit, no one comes, so they proceed to check the house to look for more of these supernatural beings.

It's a two-story home, so starting with the downstairs, they begin to check each room. With no luck, they head upstairs, staying with each other as a tight group, weapons still clutched in their hands, ready to be used at any given moment.

Reaching the top of the stairs, they see the light at the end of the hallway, and what sounds like a radio is on, playing an old creepy-sounding song. Walking slowly down the hall towards the room, they reach the door; they burst in, ready to strike. They find an adult man sitting in a rocking chair, rocking back and forth as they enter. They pounce on him, striking him with their weapons. Glenn hits him repeatedly with his axe. Mateo hits him in the stomach with his spiked bat while Amy has an arrow in her hand, stabbing the man in his neck, each striking over and over again.

Mateo and Amy are now also covered in blood, with Glenn being covered in blood already, adding a fresh coat to his getup. After they finish checking upstairs, it appears they have killed everyone in the house, so now they are setting their eyes on the next house, planning on going through the neighborhood in a circle, house by house. Once again, cleaning up the best they can, Amy grabs a knife from the kitchen to go with her bow and hides it on herself.

"On to the next house," Glenn exclaims with confidence given to him by the clearing of the two houses.

Heading to the back door, they once again head into the backyard and creep their way towards the next house. This time, there is a wooden fence separating the two houses. They hop over the fence and proceed to the back door. Locked! They continue trying to find a way in, so they check for any way in.

"Hey guys, this window is open; maybe we can get in here," Amy whispers to the group. Mateo and Glenn head over to Amy, for they, too, were searching along the sides of the house looking for a way in and found nothing. They get to the open window and stare in, but unfortunately, there's some breakable stuff in the way of trying to climb in.

Worrying about breaking something, calling attention to them, and putting them in harm's way, they opt out of going in through the window. With Glenn and Mateo having no luck finding a way in either and the three not thinking it's wise to go to the front of the house for fear of being seen by a neighbor, they devise a plan.

"What if we make a little noise out here, wait for someone to come out to check the noise, then ambush the person, rush inside, and kill everyone else?" Glenn suggests to the group.

"Yeah, I'm down," Mateo answers.

"Me too," Amy answers. "I'll go set up on the side behind the bush with the bow."

The group starts to implement their plan, setting up in various spots.

"Everyone ready?" Glenn asks his friends. After receiving the okay nod from Mateo and Amy, Glenn knocks over a metal trash can in the backyard. Hoping it would be enough to call out one of the people in the house.

A few seconds go by and a light turns on that's on the back of the house. The door opens up and an adult male comes out to look at the trash cans. Amy takes aim, waiting for the man to stop at the trash cans and pick up the knocked over one. He does, she fires, bullseye! Hits him right in the side of the head.

Glenn then comes up and slices his throat for the double tap. Everything is going smoothly and quietly, no attention is being called on them. They proceed to head into the house. When they walk in, they can instantly hear music being played. Another creepy old-time song being played on a record player. Like what they heard in the previous house. Creeping towards the music, they remain quiet, walking very carefully so as to not make any sound.

Approaching the door, Glenn peaks in and spots an adult female and a male child, just sitting in rocking chairs, rocking back and forth. Signaling to his friends that there's two in the room, they prepare to charge in and attack. With no hesitation, the three burst into the room, attacking the family. he family immediately turns into their supernatural forms before they can even reach them to strike.

Glenn goes straight for the adult, striking her in the chest with his axe, sticking it in her deep, but she just looks at it and throws Glenn against the wall. He hits it hard, falling to the floor instantly, dazed by the attack. Amy then takes aim with her bow, hitting the adult right in the neck. The being now hurt from the combination of strikes, struggling and stumbling.

Grabbing his axe, Glenn then gets up, rips the axe out of her chest and wails on her head with it, cleaving her skull in two. Blood spitting out, as the being falls to the floor, dead. Meanwhile Mateo has been wrestling with the child. Striking the being with his bat, but he is unable to retrieve it out of the little supernatural being, giving it the upper hand on Mateo. He calls out for help. Amy quickly turns her attention to the little being and fires an arrow, hitting the being in the chest.

Unfazed, the little one continues to attack Mateo, clawing at him with her sharp nails, while trying to bite at him with her razor-sharp teeth. Mateo, fighting for his life as he tries to fend her off. Amy then grabs her knife she previously obtained and stabs the little being on the side of her head, sticking the knife in as deep as it could go. Blood squirting out from the wound, directly into Amy's face.

Glenn then comes running in, shoving the little supernatural being with all his might, throwing her against the wall. She falls to the floor, still alive, but hurting. Glenn then walks over to her and stands over her as she lies on the floor, he puts his foot on her chest as he swings right for her neck with his axe. Chopping her head clean off her body. Rolling on the ground, stopping, the head pointing straight up with a grin on its face. The group is once again victorious!

After gathering their breath for a little bit, cleaning up the best they can, and cleaning their weapons the best they can, the group heads for the kitchen. Looking for liquids to rehydrate with to continue their onslaught of these horrible, sadistic beings. Upon arriving in the kitchen, they again find human body parts: an arm and a leg. Chopped cleanly off, something like what you would see at a butcher's shop. Sickened by the sight, they grab some water and head out.

Chapter 23: Mateo's Last Stand

House by house, the group traverses through the neighborhood systematically, killing each family of supernatural beings as they go. Getting better and more efficient as the night goes on. Knowing how many people they are saving, with all the human remains and body parts they find at each house, furthers their rage and desire to cleanse the earth of these foul beings.

After countless houses are cleared, countless beings killed, and still thankfully remaining undetected, the group arrives at a larger stone house. Made from the same stone that the wall is made up of and appearing to be very old, the group feels that this is the original house of the community.

"Whoa!" Amy lets out as she stares at the massive stone house. "Do you think this is like the leader or something?" She asks the group.

"I don't know, but I wouldn't be surprised if it is. Kind of feels like it would be," Glenn responds.

"I agree," Mateo adds.

They decide to be extra careful in case they're dealing with something extra powerful and creep even slower and more carefully than they have the entire night. Looking around back, they cannot find any way in; there's not even a back door someone could come out.

Just then, lights all over the property turn on, and an alarm starts to sound. The group panics and tries to run. There's a group blocking them. Turning around, they try to head back in another direction but are blocked again. Surrounded by dozens of beings at this point, some in human form, others in supernatural forms, with nowhere to go, the group fears that this is the end for them.

Just then, a tall male figure steps out of the darkness. He's very tall, not looking like the other beings in any way. He has a long gray beard, a tall hat, and a long coat and starts talking with a distinguished voice. Just like the man Glenn saw in his vision.

"We have been watching you for a little bit now. It's quite impressive for measly humans," the tall figure says to the three of them.

Mateo and Amy turn to look at Glenn begging him with their eyes to have him talk to them. Glenn explains everything. How they were kidnapped, they killed one of their friends, protecting more innocents from being killed, and wanting revenge.

"We just wanted to stop you all from killing more innocent people," Glenn adds at the end of his conversation.

The supreme being looks at Glenn like he's some puny peasant and orders his people to go ahead and lock them up. As his followers are getting ready to perform their orders, the supreme being stops them, sniffing the air. His frightening inhumane stare then fixes on Glenn, and he speaks, "I've eaten your brother."

Before the three of them could react, the mysterious knockout powder was raining down on them, instantly knocking them all out.

Chapter 24: Escape the Abyss

Mateo wakes up and looks around. "What the hell, where am I? What happened?" he calls out. No one is around, though. Finding himself in a bedroom he's never been in, Mateo looks around and begins to feel comforted, almost as if he's at home. The sun is shining bright; the windows are open, birds are chirping, a light breeze blows the curtains slightly, and the air smells like spring; fresh cooking can be smelled throughout the house. Pulling off the blankets, he gets out of bed.

Finding no more blood and no scratches on his body; he actually feels quite remarkable. He looks around the room but sees nothing that reminds him of anything. Making his way to the closed bedroom door, he peeks out but sees nothing.

Slightly skeptical but still having that overwhelming feeling of being home, he starts walking down the hallway. Checking out each room along the way, still nothing reminding him of anything but a beautiful house nonetheless. The wonderful smell coming from the kitchen grows ever more potent; it smells like his favorite pie! Growing more puzzled, he heads directly to the kitchen and opens up the door.

To his overwhelming surprise, it's Dina! Alive! He runs up and hugs her, the hug of all hugs. Never thinking he would get to hug his friend again. Holding her tighter and tighter, never wanting to let go. After a while, he finally lets go.

"How is this possible? How are you here? Where are we? Mateo asks. He has so many questions, but yet so happy to see his friend.

"You're home," Dina responds.

"Home?" Mateo asks. "How is this home? Where are Glenn and Amy?"

"They're doing what they must do. You're home with me," Dina replies.

Being so confused, Mateo returns to hugging his friend, for he's so happy to see her. He still has that overwhelming feeling that he is, in fact, home. Beyond being happy to spend time with his friend again, Mateo refrains from asking any more questions and just enjoys his time with her.

It did not feel like a dream or anything, feeling so real to him. They go for a walk outside, walking all around the beautiful country house. Surrounded by meadows and oak trees. Flowers are everywhere, and there's a beautiful garden and a large red barn. Horses run through the meadows; two little dogs follow them as they walk around while they enjoy the company of one another.

They walk up to an oak tree and just stare out at the sunset. The most beautiful sunset Mateo had ever seen, and the fact that he was enjoying it with his best friend in the world, was priceless, almost like heaven.

The leader speaks to his people, pointing out Glenn and Amy, I want those two; you can have the rest. Mateo, Amy, and Glenn now lay there, completely unconscious, their bodies so innocent-looking, surrounded by dozens of hungry, human-eating beings.

A few beings grab Glenn and Amy and begin to carry them off. The rest go to town on Mateo's body as he lies there unconscious. Jumping at him like starving rabid dogs. Tearing at his flesh, pulling his limbs off, blood flying everywhere. They aren't leaving anything to waste, quickly devouring his body to where there's nothing left but a puddle of blood. Amy and Glenn are completely unconscious and oblivious that the horrible beings have entirely consumed their other best friend.

Chapter 25: Blood and Silence

The beings grab Glenn's axe and Amy's bow as they carry them off and dispose of the weapons. They carry Glenn and Amy into the house and place them both into the same cage. Not much time passes until Glenn wakes up; he and Amy have their hands bound in rope behind their backs. Opening his eyes, then quickly sitting up to see where he is, Glenn starts to gain his composure. Assuming he's inside the giant stone house, he also begins to wake Amy up.

"Amy, Amy, wake up," Glenn nudges her back and forth, trying to wake her up. All while checking out his surroundings, looking for Mateo, and figuring out how to get them out of there.

"Amy, wake up, come on, we gotta get out of here," once again Glenn tries, all while still nudging her back and forth.

Just then, Glenn notices the knife on Amy, still hidden on her. He grabs the knife and cuts the bindings on both his and Amy's hands, proceeding to hide the knife from his person after doing so. Amy then starts to wake up. Relieved they are both still alive, they hug each other.

"Where's Mateo?" Amy asks.

"I don't know. I don't see him anywhere," Glenn answers, just as confused as Amy about their friend's whereabouts. "I'm sure he's still alive. We'll get out of this cage, find him, kill these bastards, and get the hell out of this god-awful place."

Agreeing, they sit back and wait for their time. Glenn informs Amy that she still had the knife hidden on her and that he took it and hid it on him after cutting their bindings.

"We will just relax and wait for an opportunity to make our move," Glenn informs.

Making themselves as comfortable as possible, considering they're on a floor with nothing, they huddle together and play the waiting game. All while pretending their hands are still bound, keeping them behind their backs. Hours go by, and not a single being comes by or anything.

The cage, appearing to be in the center of the house, you'd think would have someone walk by, considering the circumstances, but nothing. Still huddled up, a being finally shows up and slowly approaches the cage, almost acting as if they were there to retrieve Amy and Glenn. Thinking this could be his chance, Glenn readies the knife in his hand, keeping it hidden. They stand up together, still acting like their hands are bound.

As the being steps closer, Glenn gets more anticipatory that this will be their chance. Stepping right up to the cage, the being begins to search her, taking her focus off Glenn and Amy for just a second. That's when Glenn takes his moment to strike. Swiftly bringing his hands from behind his back, the knife clutched in one, he darts straight at the being, stabbing her straight in the eye, the knife piercing her brain. Falling to the floor, instantly dead, Glenn grabs her body and pulls her as close to the cage as possible to make it easier to search for a key to get out. Blood is still pouring out of the pierced eye, all over the floor, and slowly puddling up right outside of the cage.

"Found it!" as Glenn pulls a key from the corpse. He uses it to unlock the cage and get them both out. Knowing they still have a "mountain" to climb to get out of there, they prepare for the worse. Needing to find new weapons, they start their search.

First, searching the dead being on the floor for weapons, but finding none on its corpse, they begin to walk quietly around looking for items. They locate a fireplace which contains a sharp strong metal fire poker. Glenn grabs the fire poker, while Amy locates a heavy candlestick holder on a nearby table to use until she finds something better. Equipped with their new weapons, they set off to try and find Mateo and then to escape this nightmare. Creeping around once again, they begin to peek in each door. First checking the door closest to them, but it was just a study by the looks of it upon peeking in.

Walking along they find another door, it's the kitchen. They walk in the kitchen, hoping to find better weapons. Locating a butcher's knife, Glenn chooses to use that instead, handing off the fire poker to Amy, which she would rather use. Now equipped with a knife and fire poker, the two set off once again to find Mateo. As they begin to head out of the kitchen, a being walks in on them in human form. Startled, the being hesitates, then immediately turns into its supernatural self, allowing Glenn and Amy to strike swiftly during the transformation.

Glenn, taking his newly acquired butcher's knife, heaves it into the skull of the being. Amy, equipped with the fire poker, rams it straight into the stomach of the being. Both blows, killing the thing instantly, blood pouring out of both wounds, puddling up on the floor underneath the body.

Amy rips her fire poker out of the dead being as it lies face up, pulling out intestines with it. The two wipe the blood off their weapons best they can, with Amy trying to whip the intestines off of her fire poker and continue their search for Mateo.

Room after room, they search, and every time they come across a being, they kill it. They then head upstairs, still searching room by room, killing every being that crosses their path. Glenn uses his cleaver, slicing through each skull like butter. Amy uses her fire poker to stab and hit.

Both are covered in so much blood and entrails they barely appear huma anymore, but they desperately seek their friend. Determined not to leave without him and to take out as many of the foul beings as possible while clearing the entire second floor, countless bodies piling up as they go with their eyes set on the third floor, the top floor of the house.

"Hopefully, Mateo and the leader are up there," Glenn says to Amy. Both panting and exhausted from all the killing they've just done. They proceed upstairs, still walking slowly and creeping along as they've grown accustomed. Upon reaching the top of the stairs, they look around, but no beings are in sight.

However, at the end of the hallway, there's a massive set of double doors as tall as the ceiling. Having a feeling that's where they need to go, they give each other a look, nod, and proceed to the large double doors. Arriving at the doors, Glenn and Amy stick their ears against them to listen in but hear nothing.

Testing the door and finding it unlocked, they burst open the doors, ready to attack. It's a massive room with walls lined with books, a large fireplace with a roaring fire, countless artifacts, oh, and the rest of the beings along with their leader.

Wasting no time and raging pissed off at the sight of the leader, Glenn and Amy begin attacking the sadistic beings. They take them out one by one, professional supernatural being killers at this point. Glenn goes to town with the butcher's knife, cleaving being after being. Amy uses her fire poker like a champ, stabbing and hitting beings left and right. Blood sprays all over the room as bodies begin to pile up, the floor becoming more and more drenched with the blood of the dead.

Both work their way through the group until killing the very last one before the boss man himself, as he stands watching his people being slain. He is not phased one bit by these humans, having no fear, feeling they can do nothing to him. Glenn and Amy are soaked in blood; the only part of them not covered in blood is the white of their eyes.

"Impressive," the supreme being states to Glenn and Amy as he enjoyed the show they put on before him. "Enough is enough; it's time for you both to die," he tells them as he opens his long coat and unsheathes a large sword.

Glenn and Amy, still only equipped with a butcher's knife and fire poker, quickly look around the room at the artifacts to see if there's anything better, they can use. Amy spots a sword on the wall, lunges for it, grabs it, and quickly prepares herself for their fight ahead.

At the same time, Glenn spots an axe and grabs it, readying himself. Both are determined to take this thing out and forever rid the planet of its evil. Now ready, they prepare to fight, looking for an opening to attack. Glenn lunges with his axe; the being swipes it away with ease. While trying to strike simultaneously, Amy has her attacks swiped away as well. Both try again, same result. Again and again, they get nowhere.

The being just standing and laughing at them while they struggle to do anything against him. Glenn then picks up the butcher's knife and hurls it as hard as he can directly at the being's head. Once again, the being swipes the blade away. While distracted with the thrown knife, however, Amy goes low on the leader with her sword, swiping at both his legs and slicing both legs wide open.

The being lets out a loud, animalistic roar as he's stuck. They've finally hurt him! Taking advantage of it being hurt, they start attacking as hard and fast as possible. The being swiping some shots away, but others are landing. Slowly, they start hurting him more and more.

The colossal being finally falls to his knees, still trying to fend off Glenn and Amy. Both are still fighting for their lives; some attacks are getting through, and some are getting blocked. The being can fight no more, hurt and defeated; he finally gives up.

"Please spare me. I'll leave this country, never to return," he pleads with them, placing his sword on the ground. Covered with deep wounds and blood, the being remains on his knees, breathing heavily from the battle and the countless wounds he suffered by their hands. His wounds, deep and bleeding, which would have killed any normal human, even large, strong, battle-hardened ones, yet he kneels there, waiting for his fate, which is now in Glenn and Amy's hands.

"If we let you live, will you leave this country and never return? Your people are dead. There's nothing left for you here." Standing over him, Glenn explains his demands in exchange for the being's life.

The leader lowers his head in defeat and replies, "I will."

Glenn and Amy both lower their weapons since they've now won. Standing there and staring, Glenn contemplates what he will do with this thing before him. After a few seconds, Glenn makes up his mind and agrees to let the being live.

Nodding his head as if saying thank you, the supreme being slouches over, barely holding himself upright on his knees. Out of nowhere, Glenn takes his axe and swings it with all his might, striking the being straight on his neck, chopping his head clean off with one strike.

"I don't believe you. This was for Dina," Glenn exclaims while standing over the decapitated body, dropping his axe at his feet, officially claiming victory!

Glenn and Amy then turn and look at each other, breathing hard after a few seconds, they hug each other like no other hug ever, squeezing each other as hard as they can, so happy to both still be alive. Neither one can believe they did it. They defeated this thing. After embracing the victory for a short while, holding each other, they realize they're still not done. Mateo still needs to be located and rescued. Hoping to find clues, they decided to head to the last place they saw him, out back, where they all got caught.

The couple heads towards the front door, traversing through the house of death suffered by their very hands. Upon reaching the front door, they open it up, feeling the fresh air on their blood-soaked bodies. Feeling freedom now that all these beings are dead and there's nothing more to fear. After taking a few seconds to breathe in the fresh air, they head into the backyard.

Amy begins to scream at the top of her lungs at the sight they walk upon. Blood is everywhere where the three of them once stood when they were knocked out and taken. Mateo's clothes, scattered all over, are entirely covered in blood, along with pieces of him. His scalp and bones lay amongst his puddled remains. Glenn, too, drops to his knees and begins to mourn his fallen friend. Amy walks over to him and puts her hand on his shoulder to console him. Both remain there, silent, not believing that not only did they lose Dina, but now Mateo too. A short time passes, and Glenn decides to call the cops once again. This time, they are very confident that they'll believe their story due to the countless nonhuman corpses that litter this entire gated community.

The sun is now beginning to rise as the cops show up and begin to look around at all the mayhem. Finding countless human remains amongst all the dead, while the police apologize to Glenn and Amy for never believing them in the first place while also congratulating them on a job well done. They can see the hell the two must've gone through to make it through the night.

After being checked out and cleared by the paramedics, Glenn approaches Amy and starts to hug her, leading to a kiss. Both are so happy to have made it out alive together. Knowing that they will always remember their fallen friends.

Chapter 26: Three Years Later

"Argh! It hurts so bad," Amy yells out in pain.

"I can't believe you did this to me again," she yells at Glenn, who's standing over her, holding her hand.

Wishing there was something he could do to make his wife feel better. All he can do, though, is stand there while the doctors do their thing while Amy gives birth to their second child. Glenn's father is sitting out in the waiting room with his two-year-old grandson as they wait for the birth.

"Here she comes," the doctor says.

"You have a new beautiful baby girl, you two," the doctor pulls the newborn baby out of Amy, showing them their new baby girl.

One of the nurses then takes the newborn to be cleaned, asking for a name. Glenn and Amy just look at each other, with no planning or thought whatsoever, for they know the perfect name for their brand-new baby girl, Dina. After a short bit of holding and admiring her, Glenn's father comes into the room with his grandson so they can see the new baby.

Holding the baby, Glenn turns to his son. "Look, Mateo, it's your new baby sister, Dina. Can you say hi to Dina!"

The next day, Amy and Glenn bring their new baby girl, Dina, home from the hospital, eagerly awaiting the start of the rest of their lives, now living far away from the town where everything happened. Never dwelling on the past but only looking to the future for these two. Glenn finished going to school and went on to become a high school history teacher. Amy teaches archery and couldn't be happier with their life with their two children, never forgetting their fallen friends, and doing the best they can to live fulfilling lives in their honor.

One month later

Frantically looking around for their disc golf stuff, Glenn and Amy try to gather up everything, and they plan to take their new baby girl out disc golfing for the first time. Now that they live far away from where they once lived, they have an all-new set of disc golf courses to try out. After checking out a few courses already over the past few years, today's the day they take their new daughter to their favorite course in the area. So, they load up and drive a few blocks to the new course.

It's a beautiful day out, with hardly a breeze, and in the mid-70s, perfect disc golf weather. Many disc golfers are out on the course, having a great time and enjoying the day themselves, for nothing is better. Amy and Glenn then gather their stuff and put the kids in the stroller, setting off to start their round.

Hole after hole, they are having the time of their lives, not even caring if they're doing well or not. Nothing could be better than having fun, being alive, and enjoying their new family.

They're even teaching their son Mateo to disc golf, hoping, with maybe a little bit of wishing, that they have a future world champ on their hands. Or perhaps a brother and sister combo to be world champs!

About halfway through their round, Glenn turns to Amy and reminds her that this is the very course where he proposed 3 years before. He had heard about this crazy disc golf proposal idea from his favorite world champ, Kyle Rudd, and did the same thing with Amy.

One day, when Amy was disc golfing with her friends, Glenn put his plan into action. He followed her group, staying unnoticed, and waited for the perfect time. See, he needed Amy to have a near-miss ace on a blind hole, for that's what the whole proposal's idea is based on. That moment finally came on hole 12; Amy had a near-miss ace. So, at that very moment when Amy's disc was getting ready to land, Glenn smacked the chains with his hands, simulating an ace sound.

In the distance, he can hear Amy and her friends shouting joyfully, thinking Amy just got an ace. Glenn sat in the bushes, hidden, waiting for Amy to come claim her disc from the basket. She runs up to it, but the basket has no disc. Instead, it's a little box. Approaching the basket even closer, she notices it's not just any box; it's a jewelry box.

Picking up the box, she opens it up to discover a beautiful engagement ring nestled safely within. Very confused, she turns around. Only to find Glenn directly behind her, already on one knee. He takes the box from Amy's hand and holds it out to her, "Will you marry me?" he asks. Immediately crying and beyond happy, Amy says, "Yes."

As they continue their round with their kids, enjoying life and just enjoying the company of each other, they reach hole 18, the final hole on the course. It's one of the easier holes on the course, being a 180-foot par3, where the basket is slightly left at the end of the fairway. Giving anyone with a right-hand backhand an easy ace runs every time.

Glenn pulls out his favorite disc, a Prodigy 500 F3 with a custom Sasquatch stamp, steps up to the tee pads, lines his shot up, winds up, throws! It's a perfect throw, right out of his hand, heading straight towards the basket. The disc is spinning and flying perfectly through the air as it approaches its destination. Smash! Right into the chains, as the disc finishes its flight, settling in the bottom of the basket.

"ACE BABY!" Glenn yells out beyond excited for the beautiful shot he just threw. Amy runs up and hugs him, giving him the biggest kiss while little Mateo claps for his daddy, and even their newborn baby Dina gives a big smile.

They finish out the hole, still excited for the ace, and head to their minivan to head home for the day. Both Glenn and Amy grab a child to put them in their car seat, getting ready to head out. As they're doing so, a car drives by; being in a friendly area, everyone waves, so Glenn and Amy both stop to wave at the driver as they go by.

Just as the vehicle goes by them, the driver turns and looks at both of them, giving them the same sinister look the beings from three years ago used to give them. Sending chills down both their spines instantly, they turn and look at each other while rolling their eyes. "Oh damn, not again."

Appendix A: A Basic Disc Golf Guide

Disc golf is an adventure that combines the strategy of golf with the laid-back fun of tossing a frisbee (but we call it a disc for copyright reasons). It is easy to learn, affordable to play, and gets you outside enjoying fresh air and good vibes. Whether you are competitive or just looking for a new way to relax at the park, disc golf delivers. In this guide, we will cover where it started, what it is all about, how to play, the basic rules, and how you can get started today.

Where Did Disc Golf Come From?

Disc golf might seem like a new trend, but it has been around for a long time. The earliest versions started in the 1920s when people tossed makeshift discs at random targets. The modern version began to take shape in the 1960s. George Sappenfield, a California recreation counselor, organized one of the first official games using trees and trash cans as targets. The sport really took off when "Steady" Ed Headrick entered the scene. Known as the father of disc golf, he patented the chain-and-basket target in 1975 and founded the Professional Disc Golf Association (PDGA). Thanks to his vision, disc golf grew from a backyard activity into an organized sport that is played worldwide.

What Is Disc Golf All About?

Disc golf is like regular golf, but instead of using clubs and balls to aim for holes, you throw discs into a basket. The goal is simple: finish the course in the least number of attempts possible. Courses can be easy or challenging, often using trees, hills, and water hazards to keep things interesting. One of the best parts is how accessible it is. Most courses are free and all you need are a few discs. It is a great way to exercise, enjoy nature, and spend time with friends.

How to Play Without Overthinking It (QuickStart Guide)

1. **Start at the Tee Pad:** Throw your disc toward the basket from the starting area.

2. **Move to Your Disc:** Wherever it lands, that is where you throw from next.

3. **Hit the Target:** Get the disc into the basket in as few throws as possible.

4. **Keep Score:** The lowest total score wins.

   That is all it takes. You are officially playing disc golf.

The Basic Rules Everyone Should Know

- **Who Throws First?** On the first hole, pick randomly. After that, the player with the lowest score from the previous hole goes first.

- **Play It Where It Lands:** No moving your disc closer to the basket.

- **Stay In Bounds:** If your disc lands out of bounds, add one penalty throw and continue from the last in-bounds spot.

- **Putting Rules:** When you are within 10 meters of the basket, you cannot step past your disc until you have established balance after the throw.

The PDGA has a full rulebook for competitive play, but these basics will work for casual rounds.

Why the Disc Golf Community Is Amazing

One of the best things about disc golf is the community. It is full of friendly, welcoming people who love to share the game. There are casual rounds, league play, tournaments, and even charity events. Whether you are learning from experienced players or helping a newcomer, the focus is on fun and connection as much as competition.

How to Get Started Today

- **Grab Some Discs:** Start with three basic discs: a driver for long throws, a midrange for controlled shots, and a putter for short, accurate throws. Starter sets usually cost around $20 to $30.

- **Find a Course:** Use apps like UDisc to find a course near you. Most are free to play.

- **Learn the Basics:** Watch tutorials, join a clinic, or play with someone who knows the game.

- **Practice:** Work on your grip, stance, and follow-through to improve distance and accuracy.

- **Join the Community:** Look for local leagues or online groups. Meeting other players is a great way to learn and have fun.

About the Author

Eric Mullaly spent 25 years throwing discs, running a disc golf retail shop for 12 of them, and, without fail, hitting at least one tree a month. After retiring from competitive play and closing the doors on retail, Eric traded in his tournament weekends for new adventures in entrepreneurship, publishing, and storytelling.

He started with laughter in his debut book, *Throw, Laugh, Repeat: Disc Golf Humor, Stories, Stats, & Tips*, a lighthearted look at the game he loves. Then came *I Have Discs, Get in Van*, a wild comedy-horror ride where disc golf gets deadly. And it gets even deadlier in his upcoming dystopian thriller, *The Path of Champions*, where the stakes aren't just about winning. They're about surviving.

When he's not writing, Eric enjoys the chaos and joy of a blended family with five amazing kids (ages 8 to 27), two lovable dogs, one grumpy cat, and Emily, the most incredible wife and partner in life, mischief, and business.

From laugh-out-loud humor to dark, twisted thrillers, Eric writes stories that entertain, surprise, and stay with you long after the last page. And if you're curious about what's next, just know this: the discs may disappear, but the twists definitely won't.

Connect with the Author

Thanks for picking up *I Have Discs, Get in Van*! If this bizarre, meme-inspired ride made you laugh, cringe, or question your life choices (in the best way), let's keep the fun going!

Follow Eric Mullaly on Facebook
Get sneak peeks of upcoming books, behind-the-scenes chaos, and bonus content you won't find anywhere else.
Facebook.com/EricMullaly

ALSO, BY ERIC MULLALY:

Throw, Laugh, Repeat: Disc Golf Humor, Stories, Stats, & Tips: Your ultimate companion for laughs on the course, a hilarious collection of jokes, tales, and tips that every disc golfer needs.

I Have Discs, Get in Van: (That's this one!) A comedy-horror mashup born from the depths of disc golf meme culture. Equal parts absurd and dark, it's a trip you won't forget.

COMING SOON:

The Path of Champions: In a fractured future where society is broken and survival is a game; disc golf becomes deadly. The tournament is live. The stakes are life or death. Win, and you join the elite. Lose, and you vanish forever.

Are you ready to step onto the course?